LIFE INTERRUPTED

CIN MEDLEY

MED'S PUB
PUBLISHING

Life Interrupted

CIN MEDLEY

The characters in this book are not real people. They have been made up. They are by no means related to or pertain to anyone.

This material is copyrighted, any use of any portion of this book cannot be used without written permission from the publisher.

Published by: Med's Pub Publishing
Copyright © 2020 Cin Medley
All Rights Reserved
ISBN-13: 978-1-7342690-6-2
Cover Design by: Amanda Walker
P.A. and Design Services
Photograph by: Jean Maureen Woodfin at JW Photography Cover Photos
Cover Model: Alfie Gordillo
Edited and Proofed by: Kendra Gaither at Kendra's
Editing and Book Services
Formatting by: Med's Pub Publishing

This book was inspired by the cover.
They say that a picture says a thousand words.
Well the cover said 64,500 words to me.
And I want to thank Alfie Gordillo, for being him.
He helped me with the story, shared his brothers
name, and taught me about Sugar Skulls.
Alfie, no matter how much you think he got the better name, by being you,
you inspired me to write words that wouldn't have otherwise come to me.
Thank you. I hope I did the photograph justice.
I adore you.

I need to thank Jean Woodfin for her extreme talent. In her ability to capture
hidden moments with a click of her finger. Your eyes amaze me at what they
see, and how they unfold in your photographs. I am so proud to call you my
friend.
Thank you

CHAPTER ONE

The drive out to the cabin was one he could do with his eyes closed. Marco hadn't been back since they left a year ago. The closer he got, the harder and faster his heart raced. He spotted the tops of three wooden crosses on the side of the road. "What the fuck," he whispered as he pulled his truck over. He looked in the side mirror as the screams echoed in his mind. The sound of twisting metal, and then the silence. His breathing became erratic; the ringing in his ears hurt.

Marco opened his door and fell out, hitting the pavement on his hands and knees, struggling to breathe. He was going to pass out. Closing his eyes, he covered his ears with his hands and laid down. The world went black.

When he opened his eyes, snow was falling from the sky. He was shivering from the cold, and the silence was almost unbearable. As he rolled onto his side, the tears came. The pain seared through him like a knife with a thousand tiny blades, cutting him deep in the silence.

Taking deep breaths and gathering himself up, he stood and looked down the road. The tops of the three crosses were barely visible. He wasn't sure what he felt. Rage, anger, fear, pain—a myriad of emotions rocked his soul as his feet moved, propelling him down the road toward them. When he reached the crosses, his first instinct was rage; he wanted to rip them from the ground. He just stood there staring at them. The cry that came from deep within echoed off the silent valley that lay before him. Dropping to his knees, his sobs shook his body. He knew he couldn't disgrace their memory. Those crosses represented the end, an end he wanted no part of. They were headstones for the three people he held closest to his heart. They were his life.

"I love you," he whispered to the wind. Standing, he walked back to his truck and continued to the cabin with a backward glance to the place where he had lost his dreams. It was time for him to put them to rest. He knew Katherine would be disappointed in him if he didn't move on.

The road leading to the cabin hadn't been plowed. If he didn't already know the path he was traveling by heart, he wouldn't have seen it. No one had been here in a year. There were no signs of life, simply because there was no life left to live there.

Marco slowed as he made his way down the long, snow-covered drive, just like it was a year ago. He pulled up to the cabin, the memory slamming into him hard.

"Daddy, come on! We're going to hang the stockings by the fireplace."

Angela, his beautiful little girl, with her head full of long brown curls, just four-years-old, pulled him by the hand through the kitchen to the living room. His wife Katherine stood by the tree holding her very round belly. She was pregnant with their son. She smiled at him as he let go of Angela's hand to cradle his unborn child. Smiling at Katherine, he kissed her. "You are so beautiful."

Laughing, she smiled. "I'm fat, that's what I am. This baby better come out soon. I swear, Marco, he is going to burst through my stomach."

Bending down, he kissed her belly. "Be nice to your momma, little one." Katherine touched his bald head, and his eyes locked with hers as he stood and kissed her. "I love you," he whispered on her lips.

"Daddy, here," Angela called out. As he turned toward her, she handed

2

him his Christmas stocking. Smiling, he took the stocking, hanging it on the fireplace. Angela handed him Katherine's and then hers. "Daddy, we don't have one for the baby." Her smile dropped.

Touching her cheek, he sweetly said to her, "Mommy has something for you."

He watched as Angela turned to her mother, who handed her another stocking with the baby's name on it. "What does it say, Mommy?"

Squatting down, Katherine smiled at her. "It says Joseph. That's your baby brother's name."

Marco felt his heart fill with more love as he watched his daughter's face light up, looking at Katherine's belly. Her tiny hands pressed on her belly. "Baby Joseph." Nodding, Katherine smiled as she ran her fingers through Angela's hair. "I'm having a baby brother."

Laughing, Katherine told her, "Yes, my love, you are having a baby brother."

Angela spun around, looking at him with her big blue eyes. "Daddy, hang baby Joseph's stocking."

Smiling, Marco took the stocking from her chubby little hands and hung it next to hers. "There we go. Now, the only thing left to do is put the star on the top of the tree. You ready?"

She nodded, her head of curls bouncing. Marco helped Katherine stand. As she did, her hand moved to her stomach, and she cried out in pain, "Marco!" Her legs buckled, and the floor was suddenly soaked. "The baby's coming."

Laughing, he helped his wife to a chair. "Well, I guess we are having us a Christmas boy. Here, you sit while I get the bag."

She nodded, looking at Angela. "Sweetie, run and get your coat, hat, and gloves. Daddy will help you with your boots."

Angela and Marco moved through the cabin. He grabbed the bag they had packed and Katherine's coat, then helped Angela with her boots. Moving to the tree, he unplugged the lights. As they headed out, he turned to look at the room, smiling. When they returned, their family would have grown. Marco never imagined his life would be this complete. This full.

~

He felt his tears as they slid down his cheeks. His heart had been broken for over a year, empty with no life. Just as the cabin in front of him was. Empty. The memory of the day his life ended continued.

∽

"Come on, Daddy! We are having a brother."

"I'm coming, sweetheart. I need to help Mommy." His smile widened as Katherine puffed out small breaths.

"Marco, are we going to make it?"

Laughing, he kissed her temple. "You're the one in labor. Are we going to make it?"

She half-laughed, half-grimaced through another mild contraction as he helped her into the truck. "I suppose, if worse comes to worst, you can deliver him."

Pulling her seatbelt across her lap, he mused, "Won't that be a story to tell him when he's older?"

She grabbed his face, kissing him. "I love you, husband. Now, strap our daughter in and get me to a hospital."

∽

Marco touched his fingers to his lips. That was the last time he kissed his wife. The last time he felt her love. "God, Kate, I miss you so goddamn much. I'm so sorry."

∽

Shutting her door, he opened the back door and buckled Angela in. "You ready, sweetheart? We are going to have our baby brother."

She nodded her head. "Yes, Daddy. I can't wait to meet him."

He wiggled his eyebrows at her. "Me neither."

Closing the door, Marco made his way around the truck. The snow was falling, the air still. It was so quiet. Looking at Katherine, he smiled. "You ready?" When she looked at him, he saw the worry in her eyes. His hand cradled her face. "We'll be fine."

The road was covered with about a foot of snow, so he turned on the four-wheel drive. Slowly, they made their way through the back roads to the highway. Smiling, he said to Katherine, "See, the plows have been through. We'll be fine."

Angela piped in from the back, "Daddy, I'm ready to meet my brother."

The drive would have taken just twenty-five minutes once they reached the highway, but fate had another route for them. Marco hit a patch of black ice on the highway while doing fifty-five. There was no controlling the truck. His hand reached out and grabbed Katherine's as the truck spun out of control. Angela was screaming in the back seat. He could hear Katherine screaming just as everything came to a stop.

Days later, the fog started to lift, and his eyes opened to a white room, a room with strange noises in it. There was a murmur of voices, the ever so slight clinking of metal. Turning his head was difficult, and he was having a hard time breathing. A hand touched him, and he knew immediately it wasn't Katherine; he knew her touch. A tear seeped out; he felt the warmth of it on his face as it trickled down the side.

"Marco," he thought he heard, but his eyes closed again. He knew in his heart that his life was over, changed forever.

As he sat looking at the empty cabin, he could still hear the glass breaking, the sound of the metal bending. He felt the ache in his bones as they broke. The screams of his beautiful wife and daughter were silenced. Just like today, as he sits in the quiet, there was nothing, no sound after. Only in his mind do they live. The only sound now is his own heartbeat, echoing in his ears.

Looking at his hands for the blood he believed should be there, he only saw weathered, rough, shaking hands. Lifting his eyes to look at the cabin, he knew he needed to come to peace with this. He needed to be able to do the one thing he hadn't been able to do in a year, and that was to breathe.

Pulling the truck closer to the cabin, he shut the engine off and sat there looking at the windows. He could see the barren tree with the ornaments still hanging on the needleless branches. Opening the door, Marco stepped out into the snow that was nearly to his knees; it had to be at least two feet if not more. He walked around the back of the truck, moving toward the lake. He wasn't sure he was ready for the ghosts inside the cabin yet.

He walked to the bench he had built when Katherine was pregnant with Angela. Using his boot, he cleared off the snow and sat down. His eyes were drawn to the silent, vast, snow-covered lake. His eyes fluttered shut as the tears came. As he let go of the pain in his chest, his scream echoed off the lake. His whole world disappeared. He shook his head. "I should have known better," he whispered. "I should have fucking known better." He knew the memories lay a hundred feet behind him. He struggled to stand, so he sat there as he labored to breathe, knowing that he needed to do this. It was the only way he would be able to move forward.

Waking from yet another drunken night, he sat there on the couch in the silence, the silence he hated with all that he was.

Looking around the blurry room, he dropped his head back on the couch and let the tears slide slowly down the sides of his face. The quiet sent him to the brink of madness. He was thankful for the alcohol, thankful for the numbness it brought him. Thankful for the warmth it brought him. Thankful for the way it made him sleep.

When he finally opened his eyes, the light made his head throb. He almost loved the pain of a hangover; at least it was something he could feel. Forcing himself up, he stumbled to the bathroom. Standing there pissing, he raked his eyes over the sink where Angela's little soaps were.

"Look, Daddy. Mommy bought me my own soap."

Marco nodded, mumbling to himself. "I see them, sweetheart. I see them every day."

Making his way to the kitchen to make coffee, he searched the cabinet for something to stop the pounding in his head.

When he grabbed his cup, his eyes drifted to the calendar on the wall. It stopped him short when he realized that he had done nothing in a year but wallow in his own self-pity. Written on the calendar in Katherine's handwriting was 'Cabin for Christmas.' She had two weeks blocked off.

Now, he sat on the bench he built for them, wanting, wishing Katherine were sitting with him. "I love you, beautiful. I'm so sorry. I miss you all so much." His voice sounded hollow, dark, full of regret and pain.

Standing, he wiped his face. Stuffing his hands in his pockets, he walked back to the cabin. "I have to do this. I have to say goodbye to them." Pulling out the keys, he slowly unlocked the door, stomping the snow off his boots before he took that first step inside.

His steps felt like he was wading through mud. He came to a stop at the entrance to the living room, he leaned against the wall for fear of passing out. His breathing became erratic, his mouth dry. He wanted a fucking drink. He wanted it all to be a horrible dream, but it wasn't. It was his reality, his new reality of broken dreams. His mind clouded over, so full of the last happy moments of his life, of their life together. The last peaceful moments.

The tears fell from his eyes as the room came back to its lifeless color. The needles from the tree they had picked out, that he cut down, covered the floor. The unwrapped presents still sat under the tree. The stockings still hung on the fireplace. The star, still wrapped neatly in its box, waited on the chair to be put on the top of the now lifeless tree. The myriad of colorful ornaments still hung on the bare branches, although some of them lay broken on the floor. Outside, the snow fell heavier, blanketing the world in beautiful silence. The ghosts began to move as the last moments of their lives played out again and again in his memories. The excitement, the love, the tender touches. The warmth of the fire, the music playing in the background. The giggles, the laughter, all of it was still so fresh in his mind.

Taking a deep breath, he knew he needed to clean the place up. He needed to carefully put her ornaments away to preserve them; for what, he didn't know. Maybe her stepmother would want them. He hadn't been a good son-in-law since that day. Hell, he hadn't been a good anything. Not a good man, not even a good human. He worked, drank, slept, and woke up and started over. He wasn't living. He was slowly dying while walking around pretending to be a part of the land of the living when, in reality, he just wanted to be with them. Why had he survived? He didn't understand the reason.

Marco forced himself to move across the room. He cleaned out the fireplace, loaded it with new logs, and started a fire. He may have felt dead inside, but he was freezing. He forced himself to go upstairs but avoided the bedrooms, instead walking into the storage room to get boxes. For over an hour, he carefully took the ornaments off the tree, gently wrapping each one, setting aside the ones he was sure Katherine's stepmother would want. When he finished, he carefully took down all the decorations, placing each item carefully in the marked boxes.

It was when he got to the stockings hung by the fireplace that his heart thundered. His fingers touched Angela's. God how he missed the way his daughter smelled, her sweet curls that bounced when she ran through the house. Her pictures still hung on the fridge at home. Taking it down, he brought it to his lips and gently kissed it. "I'm so sorry, sweetheart. Daddy loves you." Placing it in the box, he turned to touch his son's, tracing his fingers over his monogrammed name. "Joseph." Tears continued to flow down his cheeks. His son who he'd never had the chance to meet, the son he never got to hold. Taking the stocking down, he held it to his heart. "I'm so sorry, son. So very sorry. I love you."

Reaching for Katherine's stocking, his sobs came. His beautiful wife, her smile locked in his mind. The excitement she felt when they discovered she was pregnant again with their son. "My beautiful girl. Jesus, Kate, I miss you so much. I'm so sorry. Please forgive me." He wasn't sure what he felt in the cold room, but a warmth filled him from within, almost as if she was hugging him. He pulled her stocking to his chest. "I love you, beautiful. I will always love you," he whispered to the empty room. Just as the warmth filled him, it left him.

Nodding his head, he carefully placed her stocking in the box. Taking his down last, he placed it on top of hers. He carried the boxes back up to the storage room, then grabbed the broom out of the kitchen. Marco dragged the dead tree down to the lake where he would throw it come spring.

After shaking all the dead pine needles off of the presents that would never be opened, he carried them up to the storage room where he stacked them carefully. As he swept up the broken ornaments and dead needles, he noticed a little wrapped box in the mess. Reaching for it, he sat on the stool. His name was on the tag, written in Katherine's handwriting. *To Marco, I love you.* With trembling hands, he carefully unwrapped the gift, folding the paper nicely and setting it aside with the tag. Inside the box was a keychain with his initials on one side and an engraved picture of her and Angela on the other.

His heart broke for the lives lost, for the loss of their dreams, which were now nothing but broken dreams. "Thank you, Kate." Fishing his keychain out of his pocket, he added the one she gave him. Kissing the picture, he put them back in his pocket and pulled out his wallet, tucking the folded wrapping paper and tag inside it. When he finished cleaning up, he headed to the kitchen.

Opening the fridge, he was immediately overtaken by the stench of rotting food. He bolted for the back door, throwing up. It took him over an hour to clean out the fridge and rid the kitchen of the horrible smell. When he had dragged the garbage out to his truck, he went to sit in the chair by the window in the living room.

Pulling his keychain out, he looked at their picture. They were so happy. "I will always love you, my beautiful girls. But I need to let you go. I'm not surviving like this. I need to keep moving so that one day I can join all of you. I love you." Bringing the keychain to his lips, he kissed it. His eyes closed as more tears fell. He needed to move forward.

As he looked back at the room, he knew it was time. Marco pulled the door closed. Taking a deep breath, his eyes scanned the horizon, and he whispered to the wind, "It's time, Kate. It's time. I love you, beautiful."

CHAPTER TWO

As Marco pulled onto the highway, he could feel the wind pulling at the truck, the snow coming down harder. It was like driving through a popcorn machine on steroids. Deep in the woods by the cabin, the forest protected you. Out here on the open road, the snow was wild, blowing across the road. Reaching for the radio, he turned it on, catching the middle of the weather report. *Blizzard Warning.* He thought about turning around and riding the storm out at the cabin. That would have been the smartest thing to do, but these days, Marco wasn't known for doing anything smart.

"Jesus." His windshield wipers swiped full force, but the windshield was covered with ice. He let off the gas, slowing to about thirty. He thought it might be best for oncoming cars, as well as ones coming up behind him, to put on his hazards. He chuckled to himself. "Who would be crazy enough to be out in this?" If it wasn't for the wind, it would be beautiful. Smiling, he thought about how Katherine loved the snow, but this shit was dangerous.

Creeping down the highway, he saw what he thought was a car in his lane, coming straight for him. Pulling off to the side and stopping, he watched in horror as the driver realized they were in the wrong lane. Jerking the wheel, the ice took it across the highway, nearly missing a tree as it rolled down the embankment.

"Fuck!" Marco yelled. Grabbing his phone, he called 911. "Yeah, I'm out here on highway 61, heading into Bells Harbor. A car flipped off the highway and went down the embankment. Please send some help. I'm going to see if anyone is hurt. My truck is parked on the side of the road where the car went off." Disconnecting the call, he grabbed his gloves and a rope out of the back. When he reached the other side of the road, he could see the car upside down at the bottom of the hill.

Looking around, he tied the rope to a tree and then around his waist. The snow was waist-high, but he stayed in the path that the car had made on its trek down. As he got closer, he realized the top was buried in the snow. "Shit," he mumbled and started to dig the side out with his hands.

When the window was cleared, he could see blood on it. "Fuck." He finished clearing the snow so he could open the door, but it was locked. Reaching in his pocket, he pulled out his keys, smiling. Katherine made him put a window breaker thing on his keychain the first time he brought her to the cabin. *"You never know when or if you'll need it."* "Thank you, beautiful," he mumbled. "I need it today."

Hitting the glass with the little tool, it shattered. He put his keys back in his pocket, put his glove back on, and slammed his fist through the glass. Opening the door, the person inside fell against his chest. Leaning across the body, he unhooked the seatbelt and pulled them out, falling back into the snow. Marco sat up, holding the person in his arms. Moving long red hair, her face came into view. "Jesus." She was stunning, with snow-white skin and light freckles dotted along her cheeks. He was bewildered, sitting there looking at her. "Hey, sweetheart." He shook her a little. Pulling off his glove, he felt for a pulse on her neck, noticing her skin felt like velvet. "Hey, sweetheart, come on. Open your eyes." There was no response. Marco sat there looking at her. "Who are you?" She felt very familiar to him.

Looking up the hill, he knew he had a hell of a climb to get to the road. He looked in the car and saw her bag, so he grabbed it, draping the strap across his body. It took him a few minutes to get up, then he picked her up, but she weighed almost nothing. He was a big man, and even though she was light, the extra weight was going to make this a tough climb.

His legs burned, and he struggled to breathe, but he took his time. When he finally made it, he gently laid her in the snow and collapsed next to her. He kept his eyes glued to her face, which now had blood all over it. "Who are you, beautiful?" He looked down the hill to see if he could see the plates on the car. He knew they were out of state, but he couldn't make them out. The siren's faint call sounded in the distance.

Turning back to look at her again, he was taken aback by how stunning she looked in the snow. Marco smiled, remembering the story of Snow White that Angela loved so much. The sirens grew closer. Looking up, he could see the lights as the ambulance and police pulled up. The paramedics came running over. "Are you hurt?" He shook his head, and they helped him up and then began working on her.

Marco stood watching them, his eyes still glued to her face. He couldn't shake the feeling that he somehow knew her. He watched as they pulled the gurney from the rig. Gathering up his rope, he went to talk to Charlie, the local sheriff.

"Hey, Marco, did you see what happened?"

Turning, Marco watched as the paramedics loaded her into the ambulance.

"Yeah, she was on the wrong side of the road, nearly slammed into me. She jerked the wheel and slid across the road and over the side. I don't know why anyone would be out in this shit." He looked up to see the huge snowflakes being whipped in the wind.

"Hey, isn't this..." Charlie stopped.

Marco turned to watch the doors to the ambulance shut. It was the exact same place he had lost his wife and children. His heart slammed in his chest as he fought the tears. He swallowed. "Yeah, it is." The ambulance turned around and headed back toward town. Looking at Charlie, he said, "Listen, I'm heading back to town. Let me know what happens to her. We're working out on Sanders Road, on the Callen house. I'll either be there or at home tomorrow. Hey, here's her purse."

"You got it. Take it easy Marco. Hey, for what it's worth, I'm sorry." He patted him on the shoulder.

Marco nodded. He hated that everyone did that to him. Why were they sorry? He never understood that. He was the one that was sorry. His life, his dreams, along with himself, were broken. He looked to where the car went off the road. The three crosses that were there a few hours ago were now gone. Closing his eyes slowly, he said a silent prayer.

Getting in his truck, Marco cranked up the heat and headed home. It was time to put his house to rest. To put his memories where they belonged. The road home was treacherous with the blizzard. What usually took twenty-five minutes, took nearly double that. Pulling in the driveway, he sat looking at the little cottage Katherine made him buy. *"It's so cute, like from a fairy tale. Please, honey, can't we start our life here? It's almost magical."* She was right. It was magical. All the work they did, not touching the charm, but making it livable. They had made it their home, filled it with warmth and love. Now, it was just an empty house, void of anything warm. But he knew deep inside that he needed to change that, that he needed to put them to rest.

Grabbing the garbage out of the back of his truck, he dumped it. He went back for the box of ornaments for Katherine's stepmother and took them into the house. He knew there were more inside that she would want. Walking into the cottage, he set the box on the bench he had made for Angela, so she had someplace to put her shoes on. He stood there looking at it, at the little shoes sitting on the floor underneath it. He moved his eyes to the hooks that held her sweater and jacket. Reaching up, he ran his fingers over the material. "Aww, baby girl, Daddy loves you."

Taking a deep calming breath, he headed to the garage to get some boxes and a few totes that Katherine bought on sale. *"It was a good deal, and with Angela growing so fast, I'm going to need them for her old clothes."* Marco touched the totes. He thought it was ironic that now he was going to use them to pack both of their things away. Not sure where to begin, he took everything upstairs, sitting it in the hallway.

Walking into Angela's room for the first time in a year, he was overcome with grief. Her room was filled with toys, her closet filled with pretty dresses, and he realized he couldn't do it. He couldn't erase her from his world, from their home. "Not yet," he mumbled. Marco laid on her bed to see if he could still smell her sweet scent of lavender and honey.

"Daddy, will you read me one more story? Please?"

Laughing, he could see Katherine standing in the hall. "Well, I think Mommy thinks it's time for bed. You have pre-school in the morning."

"Please, Daddy? Just a short one. Mommy won't be mad. I promise to go to sleep right away when you're done."

Kissing her head, he agreed, "All right, but you promised."

She giggled and snuggled into his side. Looking up, Marco saw Katherine standing in the doorway with a smile on her face. Her loving eyes watching them, she moved into the room and climbed on the other side of the bed. "You should be sleeping, my love."

"Just a short one, Mommy, please?"

"Well, if it's short."

Angela snuggled into her arms as Katherine's hand came to rest on Marco's head. Her fingers traced along the ridge of his ear as he read to their daughter. When he turned the second page, he looked at Angela and saw she was sleeping in her mother's arms. Gently, Marco kissed her on the head and got up. Katherine settled her under the covers as Marco turned off the little light next to her bed.

His head turned to look at the silly little light with its pink elephant base. "God, I miss you, beautiful girl." Marco reached up to wipe his tears, not realizing his hand was shaking. He needed a drink. He got up and walked to the door, deciding he wasn't going to do that again. It was time to lay them to rest, to say goodbye. In his heart, he knew Katherine wouldn't want him to live like this. He could hear her voice in his head. He remembered the conversation they had one night while lying in bed in the afterglow of making love.

Katherine turned to him, touching his face. His eyes closed. "Promise me, if anything ever happens to me that you will move on and live."

He knew she was afraid of dying during childbirth; her own mother died while giving birth to her. Smiling, he wrapped his fingers around her neck. "Kate, you are going to be fine. Women just don't die while having a baby. We had Angela, and you were fine, and you will be fine delivering this baby as well."

"I know you're right, but please promise me. Angela will need a mom to help her through her teenage years."

"I could never love someone the way I love you," he whispered, kissing her. "I don't want to love anyone but you."

"Marco, please, it's important to me that you keep living if anything happens."

Pulling her on top of him, he grabbed her thighs, bringing them to his sides. "If I promise, will you make love to me? I have to have you."

She laughed as she wiggled her core along him. "Only if you promise." Sitting up, he pushed his hand through her hair, kissing her. "I promise."

"I'm so sorry, Kate. So sorry for not keeping my promise." Picking up the totes and boxes, he moved down the hall to their room. The door was closed. He hadn't been in their room since the accident. His hand shook as he reached for the handle. "Shit! Get a grip," he mumbled. Slowly, he turned the handle and pushed the door open. A wave of emotion and memories flooded him, hitting him in the chest like a brick. The pain sheared him to the bone. The laughter they shared in the bed, the experimental lovemaking, her scent. She was everywhere. The boxes hit the floor with a thud, and he walked away. He didn't make it all the way down the stairs before he had to sit. His legs shook so bad, and tears poured from his eyes as he slumped against the wall. "God, Kate, how am I supposed to do this? How am I supposed to say goodbye to you?"

His memories of her floated through the space, slipping deep inside of him, like ghosts passing through his soul. He felt every one of them.

"Marco," she whispered on his lips. "I love you so much. How is it humanly possible to love someone like this?"

He smiled, touching her face. "If you ever figure it out, let me know. Jesus, Kate, I never knew I could be so happy loving someone, loving you."

"Can we get kinky again?" He watched a beautiful blush cover her face and shoulders. He loved that about her. When she blushed, her whole body blushed. It was so beautiful to see.

"What did you have in mind?" He kissed her.

She moved away from him; the soft light next to the bed came on. Turning back to him, she said softly, "Will you tie me up and spank me?"

Reaching for her, he pulled her to him, pushing his hands into her hair. "I would love nothing more."

"God, baby, I will forever love you." His body ached to touch her. Wiping his face, he took his ghosts, his broken heart, his crushed soul and went back to the room they shared for eight years. Standing at the door, his hand moved on its own out of memory to flip on the light. The room was every bit Kate. It wasn't frilly, hobo sheik she had assured him. Different patterns, pillows, the funky rug on the floor. Marco picked up the boxes and totes, setting them on the bed, their bed. The bed they created their children in, the bed he loved his wife in. The bed he knew he would never sleep in again.

As he went through the closet, he found the t-shirt she would wear after her shower to tease him. His mind went to the first time he saw her in it, to the first time he stayed home from work just to stay in bed with her.

~

Walking out of the closet, he stopped short, dropping his jeans to the floor, feeling himself grow hard. "What the hell, Kate," he whispered.

Smiling, she looked down at herself. "What?"

He stood in front of her. "I'm going to be so late for work." His voice was rough as he picked her up, her legs wrapping around him.

"Don't you like my shirt?" She teased him as her long brown hair fell around his face.

"You're a fucking siren, you know that?" When he laid her down on the bed, he discovered she wasn't wearing any panties. "My God, woman, look at you." He watched as her hands started at her chest and moved down to her core, her legs opening more as she pulled her shirt up so he could see that she had shaved herself bare. "Jesus."

His cock twitched as her fingers slid through her folds before slipping inside. Her back arched off the bed. "Marco, touch me." His fingers followed hers as she touched herself. He pulled his boxers down, fisting his cock. She slowly rolled over, shifting herself to the middle of the bed on her knees. Grabbing the headboard, she whispered, "Fuck me, baby. Make me sore."

~

Pulling the shirt to his face, he inhaled. Her scent was barely there still, but the memory of her in this shirt was one he would never let go of. It was the first time he had fucked her, the first time they stayed in bed all day. The first time he tied her up. The first time he didn't just make love to her. The first time it was as raw as it could get. His tears came again, and he knew he couldn't do it. He just couldn't bear to remove her.

He would never be able to sleep in the bed, which now held the boxes meant to fill with her things. His eyes moved to the dresser cluttered with her perfume bottles and jewelry. Looking at his hand, he knew it was time. Pulling his ring off, he moved to her dresser. Opening her jewelry box, he gently placed his ring next to hers. "I love you, Kate. I will always love you."

Marco gathered all his clothes, putting them in the totes along with her t-shirt. As he left their room, he picked up the picture of her and Angela that sat on his dresser. Walking past Angela's room, he went in and took her favorite stuffed animal. The only door left in the hallway that was closed was the baby's room. Not sure he could bring himself to go in there, he took his things downstairs.

He made it to the living room. Dropping his containers, he grabbed his keys and left. He needed a drink but knew it was not the best idea. He knew how disappointed Katherine would be in him for hiding from his feelings. He wasn't living like he promised her he would continue to do; being drunk for a year was not living. So instead of getting in his truck and going to the bar, he kept walking. It was freezing out. The wind whipping, the snow blowing, it was treacherous out, but he needed to clear his head. He needed to get a grip before he could continue.

Marco knew he would never go back in that room, not if he wanted to move forward. It was her room, their room, but now he was alone. There was no them, not anymore. It was now her room. There was nothing upstairs that he needed. The true master bedroom was downstairs. It was now his office, but he was going to turn it back into his bedroom.

As he walked, he decided he was going to enclose the bottom of the stairs with a door and drywall the open railings. Just lock it up and make it a shrine to them, to the broken dreams of the life they shared. Marco knew he would never sell the cottage, but he also knew that if he ever needed to be close to them, they were there in that cottage with him.

Satisfied with his decisions, he headed back home. He hadn't realized how cold he was, or the fact that it was a white-out blizzard. By the time he reached the cottage, he looked like a giant polar bear.

After Marco changed his clothes, he started to move furniture around, knowing he couldn't get to the hardware store to get what he needed to frame out the door until after the storm passed. It took him a few hours to move the furniture and his desk and clean.

When he finished, he took a tote and proceeded to collect everything that reminded him of the life he lost, the life he shared with them. Carefully, he placed each item with the greatest of care into the tote—the calendar, pictures, Angela's artwork, stray toys, the iPad they shared, Katherine's phone, her car keys to a car that would probably remain parked in the garage for the rest of his life, Angela's little soaps from the bathroom. When he finished, he took the tote and put it in the closet of what would now be his room. Taking Katherine's t-shirt and Angela's favorite stuffed animal, he carefully placed them on top of the tote. "I love you both so much."

Marco made his way to the couch, his heart broken, his emotions shot. He wanted a drink to make it all go away. He wanted the gut-wrenching pain that resided in his chest, in his heart, to stop. But he knew it was never going to happen. Lying down, he cried himself to sleep.

CHAPTER THREE

Marco woke the same as he had for the past year, alone. Sitting up, he ran his hands over his face and across his head. He hadn't shaved in weeks. Dragging himself to his new bathroom, he showered and then shaved his face and head. Looking at himself in the mirror, he saw the man he was before all of this. His eyes moved to the three hearts tattooed on his left pec. His fingers touched them, the grief so overwhelming he thought he would go mad. Knowing the long road ahead of him, he closed his eyes, saying a silent prayer asking for the strength to get through it.

For the past year, he hadn't allowed himself to feel much of anything. When the emotions started to rise in him, he would drink to wash them away. After getting dressed, he made a pot of coffee. Knowing he wasn't going in to work, he called his partner Kyle.

"Listen, I'm taking a few more days," he said when Kyle answered the phone.

"Not a problem. We shut down the site anyway. Have you been outside yet? I think we got about two feet of snow."

"No, but I'm on my way out there now. Thanks. I'll see you in a few days."

"Marco, I know you don't like it when people ask you this."

Marco cut him off, "I'm getting there. I haven't had a drink in two days, so it's a start."

"All right, buddy. If you need anything, you know where I'm at."

"Thanks. Hey, where's the tool trailer?"

"In my driveway, why?"

"I need a few tools. I've got some shit to fix around here. I'll stop by later today."

"Okay, see you then."

Marco disconnected the call and put his boots and coat on. "Time to dig out." As he was finishing the driveway, a car pulled up to the end of his drive. Turning, he saw it was Charlie, the sheriff. Charlie got out of the car. "Hey, what brings you by?"

"I'd like to talk to you. Can we go inside?"

Marco stood there looking at him, wondering what was going on. "Sure, come on in, you want some coffee?"

"That would be great."

The two of them headed into the cottage. Taking off his boots and jacket, Marco headed to the kitchen, leaving Charlie to follow. He poured two cups of coffee, setting one on the island for Charlie, who was sitting on a stool. Marco stood leaning against the counter, watching Charlie struggle with whatever it was he needed to say.

Charlie picked up his head, and the look in his eyes made Marco very uncomfortable. Chuckling, Charlie shook his head. "I'm not sure where to begin."

"The beginning is always a good place."

"Well, the beginning started twenty years ago when you walked into my office."

Marco felt something he was sure he never thought he would ever feel again. Twenty years ago, he was a scared eighteen-year-old who had defied his father and walked away from his family. "Charlie?"

Taking a deep breath, Charlie began talking. "When you told me your story, I had no idea who you were or what the hell you were talking about. You were a tall, skinny kid who looked like you had just walked out of a war zone. I remember calling the hotel and the restaurant."

Marco smiled. "I remember your kindness, something I never knew and something I desperately needed."

"I told you to go eat and get some sleep and we would talk the next day."

"I remember." Marco took a drink of his coffee.

"Well, while you were gone, I did some research into the fantastic story you told me." He chuckled. "It was like something out of a movie. I wasn't sure I believed you. But there was just more than fear in your eyes that day. So, I thought the right thing to do was feed you and give you a safe place to sleep while I investigated your story. I'll admit that as each fact you gave me became a reality, I grew more uncomfortable, more afraid of what could happen to the people in this town." Charlie took a drink of his coffee. "As you know, Elizabeth and I never had any children."

"I remember," Marco said quietly. Charlie had become like a father to him, taking him in and helping him. He had kept him safe.

"The things I learned in those eighteen hours, I'll be honest with you, they scared the shit out of me." He sighed. "It took me years to stop checking on things before I began to relax. I'm old now, Marco, too old I think to do anything more than just drive around this town."

"Charlie, I mean no disrespect, but what exactly are you trying to say?"

"We agreed twenty years ago that the only way to keep you safe, keep you hidden, was to change your name from Lucian to Miller."

"I grew up Marc Miller, not Marco Lucian. He doesn't exist anymore."

Charlie reached into his pocket and pulled out two cards. "I'm afraid to tell you this, but I think Marco Lucian has risen from the grave, and his family is going to reign hell on our little town."

Marco chuckled a nervous laugh, his heart racing in his chest. "Charlie, what are you talking about? No one has ever come looking for me. Why would you think they would now?"

He watched as Charlie sat one of the cards he was holding on the island, sliding it toward him. Marco looked at the card, then at Charlie, and fear was what he saw in Charlie's eyes. Stepping forward,

Marco picked up the card. It was a license; he recognized the woman from the accident. Her name was Shelia Evans. "The woman from the accident. I don't know her. What does any of this have to do with me?" Marco noticed the birthdate, May 18, 1985. *Why does this sound familiar?*

"She hasn't woken up yet. I talked to Doc. Her x-rays show multiple healed broken bones, all signs of physical abuse."

Marco was finding it difficult to swallow. He watched Charlie slide his hand across the island. Lifting his hand, Marco looked down. The blood rushed to his brain, his heart speeding up. His whole body started to shake. Gripping the island, he forced himself to focus as the memories slammed into him. He couldn't breathe, his vision blurring. He wasn't sure he said the word, "Fuck." He couldn't hear anything except the ringing in his ears. The name jumped off the license, hitting him hard. Beckett Angelo. His mind flashed to a memory he was sure was lost.

~

"What's the matter, Marco, you scared?"

He laughed. "You're a little girl, Beckett. Why would I want to kiss you? You are destined to marry my brother. You aren't mine to kiss."

She raised her hand, putting it on his chest. "I will never love your brother." She whispered, "He's a monster."

He chuckled like an asshole. "What, you love me?" He pushed her hand away. He watched as the tears filled her eyes.

"You are such a jerk. I've loved you my whole life."

He laughed in her face. "You're fourteen years old. What do you know about love?"

Her tears tumbled down her cheeks. "I know I will end my own life before I ever let him touch me."

Marco grabbed her by the arm and shook her. "Don't talk like that. Don't say shit like that." He pulled her to his chest, and when she wrapped her arms around him, everything got blurry. She felt wonderful. Dipping his head down, he inhaled her scent.

Beckett turned her head and kissed him. Marco changed right there, holding his childhood friend. The person that was promised to his brother. But when he kissed her, everything changed for him.

Beckett was ripped from his arms, and there was no time to react. His brother was on him, beating him, screaming at him.

~

Marco shook his head, looking at Charlie. "I suppose you did what you did twenty years ago?"

"Marco, your father has passed away. I'm sorry. Your brother is now in control of the family."

He wasn't sure how he felt about this news. "Tell me what you know about Beckett."

"I don't know anything about her. I remembered the last name from twenty years ago. When I saw it, I don't know, something told me to look. I didn't run her name; I just checked the papers and found the article about your father and brother. Marco, what are you going to do?"

Picking up her license, he slipped it into his back pocket. "Charlie, we aren't going to do anything."

"Marco, her car had a tracker on it. They will find her."

He didn't want this shit. "Can you move the car out to my cabin?"

Charlie chuckled. "We can't get it out of the ravine until some of the snow melts. But I did get the tracker off and disabled it."

"Thanks. Listen, don't do anything. If anyone comes looking for her, you don't know a thing. Call me, please, when she wakes up."

Charlie stood to leave. "For what it's worth, I'm sorry for bringing this to your door."

Marco walked over to him, shaking his hand. "You didn't do anything but help me. Thank you, Charlie, for everything."

~

Marco sat on the couch, looking at her picture, and he now under-stood why she felt so familiar to him. Putting his head back, he knew he couldn't be involved in this. He wasn't that young scared teenager any longer. He was a man now, a different man. A man who hated violence, who had loved the perfect life he used to have. Now, he had nothing to lose, nothing to gain.

He got up and left, heading to Kyle's and then to the hardware store to get some wood. He needed to do something or he was going to drink. He knew he couldn't get involved with Beckett; that's not a fight he wanted. His brother was always abusive to him. Marco was a scrawny kid growing up, and his brother Julian was three years older and much bigger. He was the star football player. The memories he had of Julian were nothing but torture and pain. Marco was the youngest of the three boys in his family. He could remember his father telling him his only importance in life was that he was the spare, in case something happened to Julian or Benny. He hated his father; he was just as cruel as Julian. He would beat him for no other reason than because he was there.

Trying to block the memories, he got to work building the frame for the door and putting up walls on either side of the stairs. When he finished, he headed to the warehouse to grab a door and some sheetrock.

On his way home, he stopped and picked up a door handle. The furniture store was closed, so he would have to wait until morning to get a bed.

By the time he finished with the walls and door, he was hungry. After making himself something to eat, he crashed on the couch, which was his routine. It had been a year since he had slept in a bed. He wasn't sure he would ever be able to do it again, but he needed to try, for Katherine. "I love you, Kate. I miss you so damn much it hurts," he whispered to the dark room as his eyes closed and sleep took him.

His dreams were nightmares of his childhood, the beatings by his father's hand, by Julian's hand. He could feel the blows, the bones breaking, his mother's screams as she tried to save him. He dreamt of her comforting him after. Nursing her own body from the abuse his father inflicted on her.

He dreamt of the screams he would hear in the darkest parts of the night. He dreamt of the one time he crept down the darkened hallway to his parents' room. He could hear his mother screaming as his father beat her, then raped her. It was his life. He dreamt of the kiss he shared with tiny Beckett, which shocked him awake.

Covered in sweat, Marco sat up. It had taken years for the nightmares to leave him. After getting up and dressing, he walked out of the house and got it in his truck. There was only one way he knew to stop them and that was to stay awake.

Pulling up to the hospital, he got out of the truck. Standing outside the door to her room, he looked in the small window at her. There was a soft light on over the bed. Taking a deep breath, he pushed the door open. He hadn't been back here since he left it almost a year ago. Slowly, he walked to the side of the bed. She looked like an angel, so peaceful. With a shaking hand, he reached over and touched her face; it was covered in bruises, and her head had a bandage on it. She hadn't changed much, though she had matured some. Her hair was red. Picking it up, he ran it through his fingers. To him, it felt wrong. She had long brown hair the last time he saw her.

Marco couldn't imagine what she must have endured at the hands of his brother. Pulling the chair over to the side of the bed, he got comfortable. He wanted no part of the shit storm that would follow her. He chuckled, thinking about the line from Casablanca: "Of all the gin joints, in all the towns in all the world, she walks into mine."

Why is she here? Is it a coincidence? Is she a ploy set loose to find me? It had been twenty years. Why would they be looking for him now? Then his thoughts moved to Katherine; maybe this was the reason she was taken from him. Maybe it was to save them from the war he would most assuredly be dragged into. Marco was sure that Julian was not going to let Beckett go. Looking at her, he wondered how long she had been running. It had to be at least four days. That is how long it took him to get here from Chicago. But Beckett had a tracker on her car, or was it even her car? Marco pulled out his phone and texted Charlie.

Who was her car registered to?

He didn't expect an answer since it was barely five in the morning. Marco looked at her hand. The knuckles were bruised, which bought a small smile to his face. She was still that tough little tomboy he remembered. He hadn't realized he'd done it, but he opened her hand to look at her nails. They were shredded, nearly to the point that they were bloody.

He heard the door open behind him. "Oh, excuse me. Visiting hours don't start until nine. I'm sorry, but you'll have to leave."

Marco let go of her hand. Standing, he turned. "I was just leaving," he said softly.

The nurse was surprised. "Oh, Marc, I'm sorry. Do you know Miss Evans?"

"No, I was there when her car went off the road." He moved to the door. "I couldn't sleep, so I thought I would check on her."

"Well, she's pretty beat up. I know the doctor is a bit worried that she hasn't woken up yet, but he's confident she'll make a full recovery."

"Thanks, Alice. If she wakes up, would you please not tell her I was here?"

"Sure. You take care, Marc."

He nodded and smiled a small smile as he left. His phone vibrated in his pocket. Pulling it out, he read the text.

Meet me at your house. We need to talk.

He responded: *Be there in 20.*

Pulling up to his house, he saw Charlie parked out front, but not in the squad car. When he got out of the truck, Charlie came to stand next to him. "Come on, I'll make us some coffee."

Charlie sat at the island, not saying anything, but his eyes never left Marco. "You've grown into one hell of a man, Marco. I'm damn proud, knowing I had a hand in that."

He chuckled. "I'm forever grateful for everything you have done for me. But that look in your eyes says you might be regretting it."

Charlie chuckled. "Not for one minute." Marco watched him drink his coffee. "The car is registered to your brother. Marco, this came across my desk last night." Pulling a piece of paper from his shirt pocket, he unfolded it and set it on the island.

Marco stood there leaning against the counter, looking at the paper. Taking a drink of his coffee, he picked it up. Shaking his head, he smiled. *Damn.* Looking at Charlie, he asked, "So what are you going to do?" He didn't answer Marco. "Who knows who she is?"

"Me and you. Marco, she's wanted for attempted murder and grand theft. She stole that car, and from that BOLO, a hundred thousand dollars."

"Did you find the money?"

"We haven't gotten the car out of the ravine."

"Do you know how she tried to kill him?"

"It says she stabbed him sixteen times."

Marco laughed. "Are you going to arrest her?"

"Well, that's why I'm here."

"What do you mean?"

"I'm an old man. My career is about over... Hell, my life is about over. If I arrest her, she'll go back to Chicago, where I'm sure your brother owns the police. She'll either go to jail or back to him."

"I've never asked you to do what you did for me all those years ago, but I'm going to ask you now. Can you at least wait until she wakes up? Talk to her, see what really happened?"

"And what about you? Are you going to talk to her?"

Marco stood there for a long time before he spoke. "Twenty years ago, my mother handed me an envelope and told me to leave. It took everything I had to walk out that door. But she begged me to leave. She knew Julian was going to kill me. I knew my father and my brother back then. For me to believe that either of them changed for the better would be the second biggest mistake of my life. If

Beckett did what this paper says she did, then she is braver than I was. She must be protected. I could use your help, Charlie. I need you to come with me to that car. I need to get any trace of her out of there."

Charlie stood and swallowed the last of his coffee. "Let's go. I'm not due at the station for another three hours."

Marco grabbed another rope and the gas can from the garage. He stopped to look at Katherine's car, and his heart hurt, but he knew she would approve of him helping Beckett. Marco had never told her about his past. He wasn't that scrawny, scared little boy anymore.

When they got to the crash site, Marco worked his way down the embankment with his gas can. Charlie stayed up top, holding onto the spare rope. Taking the keys from the ignition, he worked his way to the trunk. Opening it was going to be tricky with the car upside down. Luckily, the front of the car was pushed further into the snow, so he found it easy enough to push. He pulled out a backpack, tying it to the end of the rope, and Charlie pulled it up the embankment.

When Marco turned back to check the trunk, he saw something strange. Reaching in, he grabbed what felt like a brick wrapped in paper. His fingers brushed against another as he grabbed the first one. Pulling it out, he set it on the snow, then reached in and grabbed the other one. "What the fuck?" When he finished, he had ten bricks. Turning, he yelled up to Charlie, "Hey, empty my toolbox and send it down."

Marco put the bricks in the toolbox, and Charlie pulled it up. He moved to the door and looked in to make sure he got everything out. He poured the gas all over the car, then made his way back up to Charlie.

"What's in the toolbox?"

Reaching into the back seat, he pulled out a flare. "Not sure, but I can guess. You should get in the truck." Marco lit the flare and threw it down the embankment. He stood there watching as the fire lit. If

Beckett was in danger, Marco was going to do what he could to save her this time. He wasn't going to just leave her again.

As they drove away, Charlie asked, "What just happened?"

"I walked away from her twenty years ago. She was just a kid, but she was promised to my brother."

"As in…"

"As in, she was to be his wife. My family has a sick sense of ethics. She was the reason my brother nearly killed me. Beckett professed her love to me and then kissed me. She was fourteen years old. That's when Julian walked up with his band of friends. They held her back, making her watch as he proceeded to beat me within an inch of my life. From what you told me about the abuse she has endured, I won't let her go back."

"Jesus, Marco, are you willing to give up your life to save her? Chances are it will do no good, anyway."

"Well, Charlie, there's a difference between me and Julian now. He has more to lose. Me? Well, nothing matters to me anymore. I've got nothing to lose."

"You've got your life."

Marco chuckled. "Do I? My life died last year on this very highway."

Charlie didn't say anymore. He knew. Hell, everyone in town knew the loss he'd suffered.

Pulling up to his house, Marco grabbed his toolbox and her backpack. When they got inside the house, he put them on the coffee table. Charlie sat across from him as he opened the box. Setting a brick on the table, he looked at Charlie. Grabbing his knife off the side table, he stabbed it into the brick. When he pulled it out, it was covered in a white powder. His eyes met Charlie's as he laughed. "This is why my brother is so pissed. She stole a car full of drugs. This is a whole new ball game."

"Your brother is running drugs?"

"Don't know, and I don't care. But what I want to know is what you are going to do about it?"

He sat there looking at Marco for a long time. "As I said before, twenty years ago, I took it upon myself to bend the laws to keep you safe. I'm an old man now. Marco, this is your past, your family. I'll do what you need me to do."

Marco shook his head. "You are my family, Charlie, not them. Thank you. For now, I think we should do nothing. Did she have a cell phone?"

"Already shut it down."

"Do me a favor and drop it in the garbage disposal, or bring it here and I'll do it." Marco picked up the backpack. Pulling it open, he said, "Fuck," and proceeded to pull out stacks and stacks of money. "Well, stealing the car and cash are true. We just need for her to wake up to find out if the stabbing and attempted murder are true."

Charlie stood. "I'll get the phone and her purse." Marco watched his eyes move to the now enclosed staircase. "This is new."

"I just can't do it. I can't go up there every day. I can't bring myself to erase them. They were my dream come true. Now, I'm expected to move on, to move forward, wading through the thick sludge that is nothing but my broken dreams."

Charlie put his hand on Marco's shoulder. "I know, son. I can't even imagine. I'll be in touch."

Marco nodded. Looking at the money, he shoved it back in the bag. "Charlie, I'll hang onto this."

"Probably best if you do." His phone rang. "Yeah, all right. I'll be right over." Looking at Marco, he told him, "She's awake. I'm heading over there. Want me to call you?"

"No, if it's anything important, come by later. I've got walls to finish and a bed to buy."

Charlie laughed as he walked out the door.

~

Marco sat, trying to figure out where he could hide everything. His eyes moved to where his desk now sat.

"Marco, look what I found," Katherine called out to him. He was in the kitchen hanging cabinets while she was pulling up the damaged hardwood in the living room. They were going to replace the damaged parts and restore the old.

Marco walked into the living room. "Don't tell me the subfloor is trashed." He looked over her head. "What's that?"

"I think it's a secret compartment."

He knelt next to her. "Open it."

She laughed. "I'm not opening it. What if there's a dead body in there or an animal? You open it."

Marco laughed, kissing her. "Kate, I'm sure there isn't a dead body." He reached down, sticking his finger in the hole and pulling up the subfloor. Looking inside, he saw that it was completely sealed and big. "You could fit in the space, Kate."

"What's in there?"

"Nothing that I can see. It's just an empty space."

Kate started to giggle. "A perfect place to hide Christmas presents from our children. Can you fix the new wood so we can access it?"

He kissed her. "You want kids?"

"We have three extra bedrooms, so at least three, maybe five."

He threaded his hands through her hair, pulling her to his mouth, whispering on her lips, "Yeah?"

"Oh, yeah."

"Well, what do you say we start trying right now? That island in the kitchen is finished. I say we try it out."

"You are on, Mr. Miller."

Marco smiled at the memory. Turning, he looked in the kitchen at the island. Many times, he had made love to her on it. Even fucked her more than a few times. "I love you, Kate."

Moving his desk, he pulled up the section of flooring, smiling at the memories of all the hidden presents. Lying on the floor, he put the bricks of drugs in, then the backpack, along with Beckett's license.

Closing it up, he moved his desk back and finished mudding the walls. He knew after he sanded that he was going to have to paint. Looking around, he decided to paint the whole room. This room was all Katherine, so he took everything off the walls, keeping a few things he really liked, and put the rest on the stairs. He did the same in the kitchen. Looking around, he thought he might paint the whole downstairs. Once he finished, he headed to the big store in the next town over and bought his supplies.

On the drive back, he called Kyle. "Hey, man, I'm going to need a few more days."

"Marco, you take all the time you need. We'll be fine."

"Thanks, buddy."

"You sound good. You okay?"

"Well, I'm on day three of no drinking." He chuckled. "My hands are still shaking, but I'll get there. If I'm being honest, it's rough."

"I'm here if you need me."

"Thanks, Charlie's been coming around."

"Good."

"Okay, so I'll see you, maybe, Monday."

"Not worried about it. You do what you need to do. We'll all be here when you're ready."

Marco was unloading all the things he purchased when Charlie pulled up. He pulled what looked like a paper grocery bag out of the car. Walking up to Marco, he grabbed a can of paint. "Redecorating?" He smiled.

"I need to move forward. I promised Kate, and I've been doing a shit job of it."

They carried everything in, and Marco went to the kitchen to make some coffee. Charlie followed him, setting the paper bag on the island.

Marco handed him a mug. "So, what brings you by?"

"I brought her purse." He reached in his pocket and pulled out a mason jar full of water, setting it on the counter. "When I found the tracker on the car, I figured I should check things out. I found those in her purse."

Marco looked at the jar. "What the hell are they?"

"I believe they are trackers. Not sure. Marco, I talked to her. She says she has no idea who she is. Doc said it's common with a head injury."

Marco's eyes fixed on the jar. "If those are trackers, then Julian knows where she is. Time is running out." His eyes moved from the jar to Charlie's. "He will come for her. We are going to need some help. If he can beat her like that, then he hasn't changed. He is ruthless. I don't know anything about him or the family. We need help. We have to save her."

Charlie sat there looking at him for a long time before he spoke. "What about protecting you? Marco, I don't know the woman. Don't get me wrong, no one deserves what she has been through. But for twenty years, I have watched you grow into this wonderful man. What about you?"

Marco chuckled. "I don't matter here. Charlie, I'm hanging on by a thread, barely surviving. I should have died in the crash with them. My whole life was wiped away in less than a minute. I've been fighting with myself, with Kate, not to join them. But her words echo in my mind. She made me promise to go on living if anything happened to her. Jesus, it was almost like she knew. My life doesn't matter anymore."

Charlie got up and grabbed Marco in a hug. He held him while he cried. Charlie felt for him like a father would a son. "Your life matters to me, to Elizabeth, to every person you know. Hell, son, we all lost them. We all suffered. Your life matters, Marco. It matters." Pulling away, Marco walked out of the kitchen to the bathroom. Leaning against the door, he whispered, "Fuck, Kate, what do I do?" His eyes moved to the spot on the sink where Angela's little soaps used to sit. "I miss you both so much." He washed his face and went back to the kitchen.

Charlie was leaning against the counter. "This is just a suggestion, but Elizabeth has a cousin who works for the F.B.I. Besides killing your brother, the only way to save her, to save you, is to get them involved. We just don't have the manpower or the skills to take on the family."

Marco nodded. "Agreed, but they can't look like the F.B.I., in their dark suits and sunglasses. If we want to beat them, we have to be smooth."

"I'll go have a talk with Elizabeth."

"I know Julian will come for her himself. If she did stab him, he's going to need time to heal. It's a pride and ego thing for him, so we have maybe a week."

"I can't post anyone at the hospital. It would be too obvious."

"Yeah, if he comes looking for her, that's the first place he'll look. I can take her up to the cabin. Stay there with her."

Charlie nodded. "I'll be in touch."

Marco didn't want to think anymore, so he got to work. It took a few hours to tape everything up in the kitchen and living room. He painted the kitchen, then started in the living room. He was a man on a mission. When he moved his desk, his eyes moved to the floor, then to the paper bag in the kitchen.

Sitting on the couch, he pulled out her purse. It was uncomfortable knowing he was about to rummage through her things. But he knew he needed more information. There were basic things in the bag. Picking up her phone, he went to the kitchen, turned on the water, and dropped the phone into the garbage disposal. The noise was loud, and he knew he was going to have to replace the garbage disposal after, but it was worth it. Leaving it running, he went back to the couch.

Picking up her wallet, he started pulling everything out, laying her things on the coffee table in front of him. He noticed a few pictures, so he flipped through them, stopping short. In his hand was a picture of him. "What the fuck." He was maybe sixteen or seventeen. "Why would she have this?"

Slowly, Marco turned the picture over. On the back, it said: *To Beckett, the little sister I wish was mine, Marco* He smiled at the memory.

"Come on, Marco. Give me your school picture."

"Why so you can pretend we are lovers?" he smarted.

"Ewe, that's disgusting. No, so I can put it in my wallet." Beckett smiled at him.

"Aren't you a little young to be asking for my picture, let alone any boys'?"

"I'm thirteen. We used to be friends. I guess when boys get older, they all turn into dicks. You know what, Marco Lucian, go fuck yourself."

He watched her face, the tears building in her eyes. She turned away from him and stormed off. He ran after her, grabbing her by the arm. "Hey, Beck, I'm sorry. You're right."

"What, that you're a dick?"

He chuckled, wiping her tears. "Yeah, and that we are friends." He reached in his pocket, pulled out a picture, and handed it to her."

"What, you're not going to write on it?"

He laughed. "Man, you are busting my balls. I don't have a pen."

She smirked, handing him a pen. After he signed the picture, he watched her whole face light up when she read it. "I am yours," she said softly and walked away.

Marco leaned back on the couch. "Fuck." He had buried all the memories from back then, especially the ones of Beckett. They had been friends all their lives, that is until he got into high school and became too cool to hang out with little kids.

He closed his eyes. "Aww, Kate, I have to help her. Please understand." He put everything back in her wallet, and then back in her purse. Moving the floor, he dropped it down into the secret compartment. Putting the floor back, he went and shut off the garbage disposal then pulled what was left of the mangled phone out. Then he finished painting.

CHAPTER FOUR

BECKETT

She opened her eyes to a very bright room. *What the hell? Where am I? What the hell happened?* She remembered driving in a fucking blizzard, and then there was a truck. "Shit," she whispered, remembering going over the side of the road, the car rolling, but she couldn't remember anything after that.

Raising her hand, she ran her fingers over her head and felt bandages. Her head was pounding. Just then, a nurse walked in. "Oh, you're awake. Welcome back. We were getting worried about you." The nurse smiled at her.

"What happened? Where am I?" Beckett knew she needed to be careful.

"You don't remember?" Beckett shook her head. "You were in a terrible accident out on the highway. If Mr. Miller hadn't been out there, you could have perished."

"Mr. Miller?"

"Yes, he's the one who saved you." Then she went about checking her machines. "I'm going to get the doctor. Can I get you anything?"

"My head hurts."

The nurse smiled. "You hit your head pretty hard. Let me see what the doctor has prescribed for you."

After the nurse walked out of the room, Beckett scanned the room, looking for her things. She needed that backpack. It was the only way to get away from that fucking monster, Julian. She only hoped she killed the fucker.

The nurse came back into the room. "I bought you some headache medicine. The doctor will be in shortly." Holding her hand out for the pills, she swallowed them with a drink of water the nurse then offered, "Thank you," Beckett said softly. She needed to be very careful here.

A few minutes after the nurse left, an older man walked in. "Hello, I'm Dr. Anderson. How are you feeling?"

"Confused. What happened to me? Where am I?"

"You were in a terrible car accident. Banged your head pretty bad. No broken bones, but when we did a CT scan, it showed that you've had multiple broken bones. Some set nicely, others did not. You have no internal injuries, but there's some severe bruising. Some of those bruises look old." *Fuck! Look shocked.* "Do you remember anything?" Beckett shook her head. "Do you know your name?"

She needed to make this convincing. Crinkling her eyebrows, Beckett slowly shook her head. Tears were easy, and she reached up to wipe them away. "What happened to me?"

"It happens sometimes with head injuries. It'll be all right. I'm going to keep you here for a few days. Hopefully, the fog will clear."

Beckett watched him walk out the door. "Fuck!" *What the hell am I going to do? Everything is in the car. Shit!* She knew she'd been driving too fast, but she was so tired. She prayed a silent prayer that she killed Julian. Then she would be free, but somehow, she knew the bastard survived.

The years of fighting him off had taken its toll on Beckett. Her body was tattered and broken, and the bastard knew exactly where to apply pressure to hurt her.

She knew there was no way that fucker was going to have her. The minute his father died, he came for her. The man's body wasn't even cold when his capos came for her, dragging her to the family home.

"Get your hands off me," she screamed.

"Someone wants to see you," Petey smirked.

"This is kidnapping," Beckett screamed, which landed a strip of cloth across her mouth. "Aren't you a pretty thing like this?" Petey smiled at her.

She kicked him in the balls, and it was the resulting hand across the cheek that knocked her out cold.

When she opened her eyes, she was lying on the couch in Julian's father's office. She could see Petey duct-taped to the chair in front of the desk facing her.

"I was just debating whether or not to pour some water on you. But then I remembered what you look like wet, and these assholes don't need to see what's mine," Julian said from behind her.

Beckett pushed up, her hand touching her cheek. "I don't belong to you, Julian."

He grabbed her by the hair, pulling her back. "You are mine, and now that the old man is gone, you will be my wife."

"I'll die before that will happen!" she yelled at him.

Julian shoved her head forward and walked over to Petey. "Did he hit you?"

Beckett looked at Petey; he was scared. She knew Julian would kill him. A small smile crossed her face as she realized it would be one less asshole to deal with. "You know he did, or he wouldn't be tied to the chair."

Julian laughed. "I want to hear you say it, so when I kill him, it's justifiable." He picked up the knife off the desk.

Beckett knew this would be the only chance she would ever have to get away. "Yes, Julian, your goon squad attacked me. Your man here hit me, knocked me out. Hell, who knows what else they did to me." She looked down at herself. "They could have raped me, groped me. Who knows? You should have them all in here, not just him." She could see the rage boiling in Julian's eyes. She cowered when he flew past her to the door, ripping it open.

"Get in here, both of you!" he shouted.

Beckett didn't take her eyes off Petey. They both knew what was going to happen.

Julian had Tony by the throat. "Did you fuckers touch her?"

"No, boss, I swear we didn't. Petey hit her and put her in the car, and he brought her here."

"You are fucking lying to me. Why did it take over an hour to get here?"

"I don't know."

Beckett nearly screamed out when Julian shoved the knife into Tony's gut.

"You touch what's mine, you die." Turning around, Julian threw the knife, putting it through Joey's throat. She knew Julian was high. It was the only time he got so violent. He had all but forgotten she was sitting on the couch. She watched in horror as Julian walked over, pulled the knife from Joey's throat, and then plunged it into Petey's chest. "Fucking assholes." Putting his hands on the desk, he dropped his head.

Beckett knew if she didn't move, she would die. She was quick pulling the knife from Petey's chest. She slammed it into Julian's back, her arm swinging again and again. He knocked her to the floor, but she still had the knife in her hand. When he reached for her, she slammed it into his chest.

"You fucking bitch!" he yelled.

"Die, you asshole!" She stabbed him again and again until he fell on top of her. Beckett struggled to get him off. He was huge compared to her. She was now covered in blood, and the only way out was through the house. Looking around the room, she saw a backpack on the chair. Rushing over, she grabbed it and slipped into the private bathroom. She stripped, then washed the blood off her hands, arms, and face. When she opened the bag, it wasn't full of clothes, but money. "Fuck." She needed clothes to wear. Looking around the room, she saw a partially opened door leading into a closet full of clothes, but putting them on was a joke because they were huge. But it didn't matter. Time was running out, and she needed to get out of the house.

Looking at the back wall of the closet where the clothes were hanging, she saw a latch. Her hands were shaking with the adrenaline wearing off. She lifted the latch, and the door opened. When she pushed it open, lights came on. "It's a staircase. I'll be a son of a bitch." Beckett grabbed her bloody clothes and the backpack. After pulling the door closed, she dropped her clothes on the stairs and started down.

She came out of the secret passage into the garage. Looking around, she saw several sets of keys hanging on a wall. She grabbed a set and ran to the car. As she drove down the drive, she could see men walking around. They were all armed, and she knew none of them would hesitate to kill her if they suspected foul play. She just needed to get past the gate, and then she was home free. Well, not free. She knew as long as Julian was alive, she would never be free. If she didn't kill him, he would kill her.

Pulling up to the gate, her hands shook so badly that she punched in the wrong code. "Fuck. Breathe, Beck. Just breathe." She forced herself to calm down. Looking in the rearview mirror, she watched one of the guards walking toward her. "Fuck!" Reaching out the window, she tapped in the code and the gates started to open. Looking again, the guard stopped walking when she started driving out.

Beckett drove as calmly as she could out of the north suburbs of Chicago.

Wiping the tears from her eyes, Beckett sat up, reaching for the remote. She had no idea where she was, only that she had escaped. She was free, but still looking over her shoulder, unable to sleep. Every noise made her jump. Turning on the TV, she was flipping through the channels, when there was a knock on the door. Beckett turned off the TV as the door opened and an older man walked in.

"Good afternoon," he said. "My name is Charlie Jamison. I'm the sheriff." *Shit* "You took quite a tumble down the mountain. You're lucky to be alive. If Mr. Miller wasn't out there, things might have turned out different."

"I don't know what happened," she said cautiously, needing to play this right. She could very well be wanted for murder.

"Yes, the doctor let me know that, but I need to write a report, and I'm afraid that all your belongings burnt in the fire. *Fuck! Fuck! Fuck!* "We don't know who to call for you."

"There was a fire?" *Play this right, Beckett.*

"Yes, as Mr. Miller carried you up the mountain, your vehicle caught on fire. He barely made it to the road when it exploded."

She couldn't breathe. Everything was gone. Her fake IDs, the money. Fighting the tears and the reaction of screaming, she turned her head away from him. She did this. She knew she should have stopped. If Julian was alive, she was dead. "Thank you," she said softly.

"When you get your memory back, you call me and we'll see about getting you home. I'm sure your family is worried about you."

Beckett didn't turn to look at him. When the door closed, the tears she was holding back tumbled down her cheeks. "I am so fucked," she whispered.

She must have fallen asleep. She knew she was exhausted, and she also knew Julian was either dead or in the hospital. He wouldn't be looking for her, not yet anyway. But something woke her, a weird feeling of being watched. Julian used to break into her house and sit and watch her sleep. When she would wake up, they would fight until he would hurt her. She could hear his voice in her head. *"You are going to be my wife. I can do what I want."* He was usually higher than a kite.

When she opened her eyes, there was a bald man sitting in the chair next to her bed. She knew it wasn't Julian or any of his men. They all had hair. His shadow presented him as a huge man with broad shoulders. Knowing that this charade was what would save her, she needed to play dumb. If everything had burned up in the car, then no one knew her name. She hoped that maybe someone would help her.

"Can I help you?" she asked the silhouette of the man.

"Doc said you were awake, so I wanted to come by to ask you a few questions." His voice was deep.

"I already talked to the doctor and the sheriff."

He chuckled. "Perhaps, but I'm sure they didn't ask you what I'm going to ask you."

Her heartbeat sped up; she could feel the tension building in her achy, weary body.

"Who are you?" she managed to get out.

"My name is Marc Miller. I pulled you from the car."

"Thank you."

The man just sat there looking at her. She didn't feel scared or uncomfortable, just the opposite. "So, what do you want to ask me? I'm pretty sure I won't have an answer for you. I don't remember anything."

His eyes didn't move as he looked at her. She wanted to turn on the light, but she wasn't sure she could handle keeping up the lie. Someone was going to figure out she didn't have amnesia. Then the sheriff would probably arrest her and send her back to Chicago. All she wanted to do was get lost, as far away from Julian as she could get, but now, all her money was gone. Not knowing what to do, she said, "If you don't mind, I'm tired, and it's hard to sleep with a stranger staring at me."

She heard him chuckle. "I suppose it is." He stood. Beckett took notice of how slowly his huge body unfolded from the chair to stand next to the bed. She nearly recoiled when his hand reached over, his knuckle running down her cheek. "You get some rest." His voice was as soft as his touch. *What the hell.*

She watched as he turned and walked out of the room, not looking back.

"Shit. What the hell was that?" Her hand came up to touch her face where his knuckle left a trail of heat. Beckett had only ever felt kindness once in her life, and that was twenty years ago. Julian took it from her. He was such a monster, killing his own brother.

For years, she tried to find where Julian dumped the body; she needed proof that he was dead. But it never came, and Julian knew he could never snub out the hope or the spark deep inside her soul that she held for the man she loved. Well, he wasn't a man back then. He was just a boy, her best friend, and that monster took him from her. Just like he took everything from her. She smiled, thinking about the look on his face as she plunged that knife into his chest over and over. "That's everything you deserved," she whispered.

Closing her eyes, she struggled to sleep, her mind on that fated day. Julian's goons had held on to her as he beat his brother so badly, screaming at him that he was worthless. Finally, sleep took her.

CHAPTER FIVE

Lying on the couch, struggling to sleep, as with every night, he wanted a drink, but Marco knew there was no way he could do that. If he was going to help Beckett, he needed to keep his wits about him. What he really wanted to know was why she tried to kill Julian. Why did she end up here of all places? He had to wonder if she knew he was here, if Julian knew he'd been here all along.

He wasn't sleeping anytime soon, so he got dressed and headed over to the hospital. He wanted to see for himself if she really had no memory, or if she was sent here to find him now that his father was gone.

As he drove, he remembered the night Julian beat him, nearly killing him.

He just laid on the ground, praying he'd stop, praying it would end. That he would end, that Julian would finally kill him.

He could hear Beckett screaming, begging Julian to stop. "Please, Julian, I'll do whatever you want. Please, just stop," she cried.

"No!" Marco cried out as Julian's foot landed another kick to his stomach.

"Fucking waste of space!" he yelled. "Touching what is mine again. I told you, you fucking skinny punk, to stay away from what is mine. She is mine."

Marco blacked out after that. Those were the last words he ever heard his brother say to him. They were the last words he ever heard Beckett say. She made a deal with the Devil himself to save him, but when he blacked out, he was certain they believed him to be dead.

When he finally woke up, he had no idea how much time had passed. His whole body screamed out, and his left eye wouldn't open. He half-crawled, half-walked back to the house. His mother was in the kitchen when he stumbled in the door.

"Oh my God, Marco, who did this to you?" As she rushed to his side, he wrapped himself around her and cried.

His mother, the only person he could trust, she gave her life for him, to protect him, to save him.

She had found a way to get fake papers for him, stealing five thousand dollars from his father and secretly buying him a non-descript car.

"This has to stop, baby. They are going to kill you. Stay here." She left him in the kitchen, coming back a few minutes later, and shoved an envelope into his hands. "Go, Marco. I need you to go."

"I can't leave you," he squeaked out.

"You are my baby, and it's my job to protect you. I've failed at my job, but not anymore. Take this. There is a car parked in the parking garage by the library. It's brown. Go. Leave. Get out."

"Mom, come with me."

"No, Julian already told your father what he did, and that he thought he killed you. They are going to get your body at first light." She looked at the clock. "You have a five-hour head start. Go, Marco. Disappear. I need you to survive. I love you. Now go."

He shook his head as his mother guided him to the door, kissing him on his swollen cheek. She whispered, "I love you the most. The car is parked on the top level of the garage. Now go, and don't ever come back here. Everything you need is in that envelope."

She pushed him out the door, closing it on him. Marco stood there looking at the door, shaking with tears streaming down his cheeks.

That was the last time he ever saw his mother. A week after he arrived in town, Charlie had told him that she was murdered. Sitting in the parking lot looking at the hospital, he couldn't shake the feeling that there was a reason Beckett was there.

Walking into her room, Marco made sure he was quiet as he pulled the chair next to her bed and sat looking at her. His eyes scanned her body. She hadn't grown much. Smiling, he remembered all the times he watched her kick the ass of one boy or another.

No matter what memories he had of her, his objective must remain the same. Why was she there? Sitting in the chair in near darkness, looking at her, knowing she was awake, Marco found himself getting excited to talk to her. He was excited to talk to anyone really who didn't look at him with pity and sorrow for the loss he'd endured.

When her head turned and her eyes opened to look at him, he knew she was scared. Her words were soft, and her voice sounded the same, exactly the same. Marco sucked the inside of his cheeks between his teeth to stop himself from smiling.

She played it well; he had to give her that. He couldn't help but admire her strength and willpower. Her determination to make everyone believe she had amnesia. When he spoke, he struggled to keep his chuckle contained. Standing to leave, he ran his knuckles down her cheek. *I know you are lying, Beck. But why are you here?* She didn't flinch, her eyes looking at him. He wondered if she knew it was him. He told her his name was Marc Miller. He was bald and covered in tattoos and solid muscle, certainly not the body of the scrawny eighteen-year-old she once knew.

He walked out of her room with a small smile on his face. Beckett Angelo was right there in front of him, someone he never thought he would ever see again. As he drove home, he couldn't help but wonder why. How did she end up in this small town about a hundred miles from the Canadian border? Maybe she was headed to Canada. Marco was too scared to cross the border when he was so young, so beaten up. It's why he stopped here. The trust and understanding from Charlie and Elizabeth kept him here. He knew that this place would be his home. Katherine was his home, but they were taken from him, just like everything else. Would Beckett being here take even more from him?

The sun was coming up as he pulled up his driveway. His phone vibrated in his pocket, so he pulled it out and looked at it.

Your cabin

Marco put the truck in reverse and headed to the cabin. When he pulled down the drive, he saw Charlie's car. Two men besides Charlie got out. "Fuck," Marco mumbled as he got out of the truck. Charlie walked up to him. "What's all this?" Marco asked him.

"Come for a walk with me," Charlie said softly. They headed toward the lake. The snow was deep as they pushed through it. Charlie turned to him. "I made the call. I didn't give him any real information, just asked him to come for a vacation, that we needed to talk. The guy with him is his husband. I figured the best place to talk was here. Marco, are you sure about this?"

He chuckled. "No. I want nothing to do with this, but I went to see Beckett. I wanted to know if she was telling the truth."

"Is she?"

"No. She knows who she is and what's going on."

"How can you tell?"

"Her response to me. Her story was already prepared."

"Does she know who you are?"

"Not sure, but I told her my name is Marc Miller. She didn't seem like she knows the name. She didn't see my face really, so I don't know how much she knows." He looked past Charlie at the two men standing by his car. "I have to protect her. Julian is coming for her. He won't send anyone. He'll come himself."

"Well, let's go feel Jay out, see if he can do anything to help."

Walking up to the car, Charlie introduced them. "Jay, this is Marc Miller. Marc, Elizabeth's cousin Jay Munch."

Marco put his hand out. "Good to meet you."

"Same here. This is my husband, Christopher." Marco shook his hand. He felt familiar, but couldn't place him. "So, Mr. Miller, why am I on vacation?"

"Marc. Why don't we go inside? It's a bit cold out here."

They made their way into the cabin; Marco was hit with the ghost of memories as he opened the door. Fighting through his grief, he built a fire so they would stay warm, and everyone got comfortable.

Marco looked at Jay for quite some time before he opened his mouth. "Can I ask what you do for a living?"

Jay smiled. "I work for the F.B.I."

"What exactly do you do for the F.B.I.?"

Jay sat there for a long time looking at Marco. "I'm the head of the organized crime task force. Why, Marc? What's this about?"

"Well, Jay, my name isn't Marc Miller. Well, it is legally, but that is not the name I was given at birth. I became Marc Miller over twenty years ago when I came here."

"Apparently, I'm here for something other than a vacation. Are you going to tell me who you are?" Jay looked at Charlie.

"That depends."

"On what?"

Marco chuckled. "Oh, how upstanding of a human you are, and how clean your department is."

"Mr. Miller, I run a tight department. My men are vetted and thoroughly investigated."

"Jay, no offense, but for the nearly forty years I've been alive, your task force has not managed to end organized crime. So, I'm led to believe that either you have people in your organization who aren't who they say they are, or you suck at your job. Which is it? Because what I have to say to you is not only a death sentence to everyone in this room, but also a career-making moment. Excuse my caution, my hesitation in divulging a secret so deep that it hasn't been brought to light in over twenty years."

"Why don't you tell me, and I'll make that decision."

Marco took notice of Christopher. His whole body was tense, nearly electrified. Every time Marco looked at him, his eyes darted away. He didn't trust him. "Alone." He nodded to Christopher.

Jay sat there for the longest time before he turned to look at Christopher. "Would you mind waiting in the car?" Hesitating, he agreed.

"Leave your phone," Marco said.

"I will not," Christopher said as he stood up.

Marco stood. "Then this conversation is over. Thank you for

coming all this way, Mr. Munch." Turning to Charlie, he said, "Lock up when you leave."

When Marco opened the door, Jay called out, "Wait!" Then to Christopher, "Please, leave the phone."

He dropped the phone on the table and stormed out the door. Marco watched him get in the car. Closing the door, he looked at Jay. "Your husband is a plant."

"I'm not sure what you're saying."

"Let me guess. You met him as you were moving up in the agency. When you found out you were going to be named the head of the division, he proposed."

"Yes."

"He's the mole. When you check it out and you discover that I'm telling the truth, then we'll talk. But until then, we are done here. I'm pretty sure he wouldn't have a problem slitting your throat."

"If what you believe is true, then no matter what I do he'll still report back."

"Then the only place for him to be is in jail, where he can't contact anyone." Marco looked at Charlie. "Can you lock him up?" He nodded. Marco looked at Jay. "There's your solution. When it's done, I'll meet you back here and then, Mr. Munch, we can make you a hero. But this stays between us. No one knows." He opened the door. "Don't talk about any of this in front of your husband." He walked out the door and headed home.

After Marco left, Jay stood looking at Christopher. "Do you discuss cases with him? Do you bring files home?"

"Yes," Jay said softly.

"Do you find yourself running in circles?"

"Yes. Charlie, what is going on here?"

"Nothing. It's not my business."

Jay turned and looked at him. "Well then, the only thing left to do is put my husband in jail."

"Can I make a suggestion?" Jay nodded. "Everything you brought with you needs to be burned. Your phones need to be destroyed. The clothes, coats, and shoes both of you are wearing need to be burned."

"You can't be serious."

Charlie chuckled but not in a funny way. "Very serious. The sooner, the better. I have a jumper at the jail for Christopher. After we get him settled in, we'll burn everything."

"And this is the only way this guy is going to talk to me?" Charlie nodded. "Then let's go."

Not much was said on the way back to town. Charlie pulled up in front of the station. He opened the back door for Christopher, and when he got out, Charlie handcuffed him.

"What the hell are you doing?" he shouted.

"Putting you in protective custody."

"What?"

"Yep, I believe you are a danger to yourself." Walking him into the station, Charlie took him back to the jail. "I'm going to need all your clothes, socks, and shoes." He grabbed a plastic bag. "Put them in here. I also want you to empty your pockets and put everything in this bag."

"You can't be serious." He looked at Jay. "Why are you letting him do this?"

"He has a valid point."

Christopher just stood there looking at Jay. "Please, don't let him do this."

"Let's go, Christopher. Get them off," Charlie said.

Slowly, he undressed until he was standing in just his boxers. "All of it." Charlie handed him a bright orange jumpsuit as he pushed him into the cell, shutting the door behind him.

In the car, Charlie said to Jay, "I'll stop at the store. You run in and get some new clothes, including underwear, a coat, and shoes. Change in the store and bring out your stuff."

Jay opened the door. "Oh, and leave your phone."

He laughed handing Charlie the phone. "Buy a new wallet, too."

Marco made it home, ate something, and began sanding the drywall. His new bed was coming this afternoon, and he needed to finish painting.

As he was finishing up, his phone vibrated.

It's done.

Marco looked at the clock and texted back.

4

His bed was delivered with sheets, pillows, and blankets. He just left it and headed to the cabin. Time was running out; he knew he had to do something to save Beckett. Even if it meant sending his brother to prison. Even if he had to kill him to save her, he would.

A smile crossed his lips when he thought about her lying to him. She could never lie to him; her eyes always gave her away.

Pulling down the drive, he saw Charlie's car. They all went inside, and Marco lit a fire and sat down.

"We burned everything. Christopher is in jail, and both phones have been destroyed. Now, have I done enough to gain your trust, Mr. Miller?" Jay asked.

Marco sat there for a long time looking at him. He knew he needed help. He couldn't walk away from Beckett again. If it was the last thing he did in this life, he would help her get her freedom. He took a deep breath. "My name is Marco Lucian. I am the third son of Marcel Lucian." He almost laughed when Jay turned ashen.

"Marco Lucian was murdered twenty years ago..."

Marco interrupted him, "By my older brother Julian. That's what he told everyone. But I survived. My mother got me out. She paid the price with her life. My father was the one, I'm sure, who knew I was still alive, or at least thought I was."

Jay looked at Charlie. "How do you fit into all of this?"

"He ended his escape here. Elizabeth and I helped him. His mother had given him a new identity, so we made it legal."

"So, for twenty years, you've been hiding him?"

"Pretty much." Charlie was looking at Marco. "He's been the son we could never have."

"Marcel Lucian is one of the most violent mob bosses we've ever encountered. We could never get close to him, and you're telling me that the missing link has been living here for the last twenty years?"

"I'm not the missing link. My father is dead, and now my brother Julian has taken his place."

"What aren't you telling me?"

Marco laughed. "Quite a lot, Jay."

The two of them sat there looking at each other. Marco sized him up, trying to decide if he should trust him with the rest of the story.

Jay wondered what Marco had to offer him. This could be the biggest bust of his career. It could also land him in a grave, along with Charlie and Elizabeth. Jay spoke first. "Marco, if you've been gone for twenty years, and the family believes you to be dead, why am I here?"

"Why don't you tell me what you know of my brother Julian."

"He is as violent as your father. We know your father refused to deal drugs, but we suspect Julian does. I know someone assassinated his top three and then brutally stabbed your brother. Sixteen times. Word on the street is that his fiancé stole a hundred grand from him and is now wanted in connection to his attempted murder. We know, or at least thought we knew he murdered his little brother for trying to rape a fourteen-year-old girl."

Marco chuckled, causing Jay to look at him. "Jay, my father didn't play that way. If I had done that, I would be dead. The only woman that was raped was my mother. My father respected every woman except for her. Was my mother's death ever investigated?"

"She was killed in a robbery at a jewelry store."

Marco shook his head. "My father murdered her. She was never allowed to go shopping. In fact, she was never allowed out of the house. She was his prisoner. I think this is enough conversation for now. I'm not sure I trust you enough yet to tell you anything more. I need time to think. Where is my brother right now?"

"In intensive care. Whoever attacked him sliced him up pretty good."

"Who filed the report about the stolen money?"

"Julian."

"So, he's responsive?"

"Yes."

"When did all of this happen?"

"Six days ago."

"Jay, when did he report this?"

"Two days ago."

"Thank you," Marco said to him, then looked at Charlie. "I need to think. Could you lock up? Don't worry about the fire; it'll burn out. Jay, I'll be in touch with Charlie."

Jay nodded, and Marco left.

Jay watched as Marco pulled out of the drive. "What are you willing to tell me about him?"

"He's a good man. Owns the local construction company with his friend Kyle McAllister. He owns his house, this cabin, and the twenty-five hundred acres it sits on. He's not rich, but he's got money. Last year, his wife, four-year-old daughter, and their unborn son were killed in a horrific car crash. He spent three months in the hospital recovering. I'm still not sure he has recovered mentally from that."

"Jesus."

"Not sure how long he'll take, so why don't we go see Elizabeth and Christopher?"

Marco sat on the couch thinking about the horrible life his mother endured. For twenty-five years she was his prisoner. Beckett was the same. He felt guilty for leaving her behind. He knew, if he had taken her with him, they would both be dead.

He had no choice but to save her. But she needed to come clean with him. Pushing up, he headed to the store. She was going to need some clothes.

Walking into the hospital, it was time to face her. To see if she knew who he was. It had been twenty years, and there was no way he looked anything like the scrawny eighteen-year-old he left behind.

Marco pushed her door open; she was sitting up looking out the window. He saw her hand move to her face, wiping the tears away when she realized someone was in the room. Slowly, she turned her head and looked at him. "Can I help you?" Her words were soft. Marco didn't say anything. He just set the bags on the bed by her knees and sat down in the chair. Her eyes never left him. He could tell she was trying to figure out who he was. Sitting up, she looked in the bags. "What's all this?"

"Doc said you were getting out of here in the morning, and you need clothes to wear and a coat. It's pretty cold out."

"Thank you, but I have clothes and a coat."

"No, you don't. They cut them off you."

"None of it matters. I have nowhere to go and no money to go anywhere with. Not to mention, I have no idea who I am or where I belong."

Marco noticed she didn't look at him. He tried to hide his smile. He knew she was lying. "Well, that's where you're wrong."

That turned her head. She watched as he stood and moved to the bed. His knuckles ran down her cheek. "You're coming home with me. I'll see you at eight." Marco didn't give her the chance to respond; he walked out of her room with a smile on his face. He was taking her home and he was going to tell her everything. Then, together, they were going to take down the Lucian crime family.

CHAPTER SIX

Beckett sat there watching the huge man walk out of her room. When the door closed, she touched her cheek. "What the hell was that?" She wondered who he was and why he kept touching her.

Something wasn't right here. She didn't know him, so she knew Julian didn't send him to bring her back. People seemed to know this man. She wondered if he was married. He had to be; he was fucking gorgeous. It didn't matter. Her heart belonged to one man. It had since she was twelve, but Julian murdered him right in front of her.

She reached up to touch the tiny sugar skull she had tattooed on her chest right above her heart. Fucking Julian broke her arm when he heard she got it.

He grabbed her by the hair, pulling her up to him. "Word on the street says you marked what is mine."

"I don't belong to you, Julian," she snapped at him.

The sting of his slap across her face only added fuel to her rage.

Julian forced his kiss on her. Beckett bit his lip, drawing blood. He slapped her again, then ripped her t-shirt off, his eyes zeroing in on the small skull on her chest. He tried to wipe it off. "What the fuck is this?"

She stood there, defiant. "It's a fucking tattoo, you idiot."

Julian jerked her head back, making her wince in pain. "This flesh is mine. I don't remember giving you permission to mark it up with bullshit like this, and a fucking death skull at that."

"It's a sign of respect for the dead, dickhead."

His hand grabbed her around the throat, squeezing. "The only dead person you know is the fucking asshole that touched what was mine."

Gasping for breath, she spit out, "He will forever own my heart."

Julian's grip tightened. Beckett was starting to black out, but she wasn't scared. She welcomed death. But as always, he released his grip on her, shoving her to the floor. Her arm snapped when she landed on it the wrong way, but the pain was nothing compared to his foot in her lower stomach.

"You belong to me. You will be my wife. You will give me an heir," he shouted at her, kicking her again. "Mark what's mine again and you will join my brother."

~

Beckett smiled, knowing she went out and got a little heart tattooed on her hip. Julian would never have seen it. She would have killed herself before she let that happen.

Looking at the bags the mysterious Mr. Miller left for her, she pulled them toward her to look inside. She pulled out jeans, looking at the size, surprised to see they were her size, the same with the shirt, panties, and shoes. The bra was a sports bra, which made her wonder how he knew what size she wore. But then again, she was sure he would be very familiar with the female body.

Taking a deep breath, she was thankful that Julian never took that from her. He always said that she would be a virgin on their wedding night. It didn't stop him from forcing her to watch him have sex with different women. He said it was to teach her what was expected of her as his wife.

Hopefully, he was dead, but somewhere inside her, she knew he wasn't. You just can't kill evil like that.

She folded her new clothes as she pulled the price tags off, sitting them on the bed next to her. Turning off the light, she lay in the darkness, terrified of what was to come. The only thing she knew for sure was that she would end her own life before she would go back to the brutality of Julian. Back to being forced to marry him and then be raped by him. She shook her head. "I'll die first."

Eventually, sleep took her, but it was far from peaceful. When her eyes snapped open, it was morning and Mr. Miller was sitting patiently in the chair across the room with no expression on his face. "Bad dreams?" he asked.

"Something like that."

The doctor came in. "I have your release papers. Mr. Miller has been very considerate in volunteering to help you out until your memory comes back and you are able to contact your family."

"But he's a complete stranger. What if he hurts me?"

The doctor smiled at her. "Mr. Miller is an upstanding member of the community. The sheriff raised him. He's a good man. I can call Charlie if you'd like. He can tell you."

She looked at the doctor. "Who's Charlie?"

"The sheriff." He patted her knee. "You'll be fine. Where else do you have to go?"

"Can't I just stay here?" She was freaking out, more than a little.

"You'll be fine." He smiled and left the room.

Marco just sat in the chair, trying to hide his smile. Beckett just sat in the bed. She wasn't sure this was the best idea, but she had nowhere to go and no money. When he stood, she looked at him, "I'll leave so you can get dressed."

Watching him walk out, she couldn't help but notice that he was nearly twice the size of Julian. At that moment, Beckett realized that it didn't matter anymore. She was dead either way. Resigned to the fact that she had zero options, she took her clothes and got dressed. Amazingly, the clothes fit her perfectly. The door opened and a nurse walked in pushing a wheelchair. "You ready?"

"Not really." She got up and sat in the chair. When the nurse pushed her out the front door, there he was leaning against a silver truck. His eyes locked on hers as they approached him. He opened the door for her. Reluctantly, she stood up, and the nurse went back inside, leaving them standing there.

"I'm not so sure this is a good idea." She squared her shoulders.

"I'm not going to hurt you." His voice was full of the pain he felt for her.

"How do I know that?"

"Well, I guess you're going to have to trust me."

"Fine, but only because people know I'm with you," she smarted. Freaking out, she climbed up into the truck. She didn't do anything when he reached over and secured her seatbelt. Turning her head, she stared out the window, watching the town go by, then they were on the highway.

Fear built the farther away they drove. Wiping her tears, she tried to get control. It felt like forever when he finally slowed down, turning off the main road. Now she was really scared; they were in the woods. From what she could see, the snow was deep, and there were no houses anywhere. She looked around for something she could use to defend herself, but there was nothing.

When he pulled into a long drive, she could hear her heart beating in her ears. *Fuck! Don't pass out. Stay calm. Breathe.*

He got out of the truck, but she didn't move. Her legs weren't going to hold her up. He carried in a bunch of bags, which she believed to be groceries. On his third trip out, he opened her door. "You coming?"

She had no choice but to get out. Slowly, her shaking hand unclicked the seatbelt. He moved to open the back door and grabbed more bags. She lowered herself to the ground, looking at the path through the snow, where it was obvious that there was traffic to the door. Her movements were slow as she walked in then pushed the door shut. He was filling the fireplace with wood. "Take your boots and coat off and come sit by the fire. This is the only source of heat down here. I got you some heavier clothes." He nodded to the bags he grabbed out of the backseat. "There are stoves in the bedrooms, so you'll stay warm at night," he said as she moved into the room.

"Thank you." Her hands were shaking as she reached for the blanket draped along the back of the chair.

When he stood, she felt herself cringe in fear, just like when Julian would approach her. He stood there looking at her, and she knew he saw it. "Make yourself at home. I'm going to put the food away and make us something to eat." He started out of the room.

"I'm not hungry right now," she mumbled, her eyes not looking away from the fire. She sat there for a long time just watching the flames. She hadn't noticed that he had come back into the room and was watching her. Slowly turning her head, they locked eyes. Beckett noticed they were blue, and she couldn't turn away. Something in them let her know there was great pain deep in his soul. Just like hers.

"I need to get more wood. If you want to sleep, the bedroom is the first door on the right, past the bathroom." She watched him stand.

"Do you mind if I just lay down on the couch?"

"Help yourself."

With her mind going a million miles a minute, she tried to get comfortable. But when he finished, he sat down in the chair and stared at her.

"Why would you do this? Help me like this?"

"You need my help."

"What's in it for you?" Beckett was sure he would say sex.

"It's the right thing to do."

She chuckled. "Is it?"

"Well, I think it is. Can I ask you something?"

"You can pretty much do what you want. I'm sort of at your mercy here. But I don't think I can answer any of your questions since I don't remember anything."

Leaning forward, he simply said, "Can I get you something to eat or drink?"

Beckett was sure he was going to try and get her to confess. "Sure, both if it's not a bother." She watched him walk out of the room. He came back a bit later, while she stood in front of the window wondering what would become of her. She didn't have a phone or any way to find out if he had survived. She knew this man had a phone, but looking around, it was nowhere in sight. *Fuck* She was totally at this man's mercy.

Marco was struggling not to say something to her. He decided to buy her favorite foods, surprising himself that he even remembered any of them. But when they were kids, they both loved pancakes with cream corn, so that's what he made.

Walking into the living room with two glasses of milk, he saw her standing by the window holding herself. She was scared, but who wouldn't be? Making the decision to tell her everything after they ate, he went and grabbed their plates.

Beckett turned when he came into the room carrying the plates. It had been a long time since he'd eaten this. It was, for years, his only connection to his past, to her, and along with all the unhealthy things, he slowly put it away. Marco made sure to watch her face, her eyes when she realized what was on the plate. He could see the confusion in her eyes.

"What's this?" She didn't look at him.

"Pancakes and cream corn. It was my favorite thing to eat when I was a kid." He nearly choked when her head snapped up, her eyes giving her away. He knew right there that she had all her facilities about her. She was lying. He was more impressed at the way she caught herself.

"It sounds disgusting." She made a face as she sat down.

"Try it, you might find that you like it." He watched her struggle. When she put a forkful in her mouth, he saw her eyes roll, but she made a funny face that made him laugh. "It's not bad." She smiled. After she cleaned her plate, she took his along with hers to the kitchen.

Marco reached in his pocket and pulled out the picture of him, putting it on the table. As he was moving back into his chair, she came into the room.

"There's something I want to know," he said.

She kept her eyes on his. "I told you I don't remember anything."

"Well, here's the thing. I think, and for good reasons, that you are lying."

She laughed a nervous laugh. "There isn't anything I can do about that."

"Where did you get that?" He nodded to the table.

Beckett lowered her eyes. Marco watched as her whole body changed. In a small voice, she said, "I don't know who that is."

He could see she was hardly breathing, as she stared at his picture. "Well, then I guess it wouldn't matter if I threw it in the fire." He leaned forward to pick up the picture when her hand slammed down to cover it."

"He was a boy I loved."

"What happened to him?"

"He was murdered," she said softly. He watched her wipe her tears away. She knew she was busted. Getting up, he moved to the couch, pulling her into his arms and let her cry. Beckett pulled away from him. "Where is the bathroom?"

"The door just past the stairs." Marco moved back to the chair, resting his elbows on his legs. The way she felt in his arms startled him, confused him. "God, Kate."

"Who's Kate?"

Picking his head up, he looked at her. "My wife."

Her eyes instantly filled with pain. "Does she know that you have me here? I mean, she isn't going to come home and try to kill me, is she?"

"This isn't my home, and no, she isn't. So, you remember every-thing then?" He didn't want to talk about Katherine now. He needed to find the strength to help her.

"No," her answer was quick.

"Well, then how do you explain knowing the boy in this picture?"

He picked it up. "He can't be, what, seventeen?" He looked at her. "You are a hell of a lot older than seventeen."

He watched her hand move to her chest. "The doctor said I would get flashes of memories. So, I guess that's what happened."

"Why are you lying to me?" He nearly said her name.

"What makes you think I'm lying?"

Marco didn't move his eyes from hers. "Because I'm not dead, Beckett."

Her eyes rolled in her head as her body went slack. He freaked when her body fell to the floor.

"Shit!" Jumping up, he put her on the couch, sitting next to her. "Jesus Christ." He touched her face. "Beck, come on, sweetheart." Her eyes fluttered and opened, filling with tears. "Don't cry."

Shaking her head, she cried, "Why would you do this to me? Why would you say something like that, to hurt me?"

"Beckett, it's me."

"Who's Beckett?"

He saw the fear flash in her eyes when he said her name. Smiling, he said, "Your name is Beckett Angelo, and your mother's name is Isabel. Your father worked for my father, Marcel Lucian. The reason my brother Julian tried to kill me that afternoon was because I kissed you in the field."

She pushed up off the couch. "None of that is true. None of it."

"I know you're scared, Beck. Julian survived."

She stopped pacing. "He killed those men. He was going to rape me. I couldn't let him."

Marco went to her, pulling her into his arms. "How did you know where I was?" he whispered.

"I didn't. I thought you were dead. I was going to Canada, maybe Alaska. It was you on the road I nearly hit?"

He nodded. "We have a great deal to talk about."

"He isn't going to stop." Her whole body trembled. "I have to remain unknown. No one can know who I am. Everything burned in the fire. That's what the sheriff told me."

Marco pulled back to look at her. "Come on, sit down." He led her back to the couch, sitting across from her in the chair. "I need to apologize for leaving you. I sat outside your house that night for so long. If I had taken you with me, they would have known and hunted us both. When the sun started to come up, I knew I had to leave. Beck, it took everything I had to leave you behind."

"But you did, and you never looked back."

"No, I didn't. Today, well, five days ago, when I found out who you were, the nightmares came back. It took me years before they stopped. Years before I felt safe." He watched her eyes move to his hand, to where his wedding band sat for eight years, the mark still visible.

"You have a wife. I suppose you have kids, too."

Marco looked at his hand. "Two." But the word sounded strangled as he said it.

"So, if this isn't your home, shouldn't you be getting back? I'm sure she is worried about you." She lowered her voice. "I know I would be worried."

He stood, grabbed his coat, pulled on his boots, and walked out the door. Sitting on the bench out back, his tears came. "God, Kate, it hurts so much," he whispered, looking at his hand. His fingers traced the worn spot where his ring sat.

His guilt was deep for surviving, but now a pang of new guilt filled him. When he held Beckett, an overwhelming feeling of comfort took him by surprise. He loved his wife; he wanted Katherine. Closing his eyes, he could see her dancing around their living room, her eyes filled with so much happiness. Her laughter slowly faded as she blew him a kiss, waving goodbye to him. Her words faded in his mind, "I love you, Marco. Always."

"Always, Kate. Always," he whispered to the image as it faded to nothingness. He was shallow and empty inside. Wiping the tears from his cheeks and taking a deep breath to calm his nerves, he stood and looked at the lake. "I love you, Kate. Thank you."

When he walked back into the living room, Beckett was on the couch looking at him. In his mind, he saw her as the terrified fourteen-year-old he left behind. He had to be strong because this was a fight he needed his wits for. He knew Julian didn't hold any remorse for killing him, and he needed to let all his past demons surface because, in the end, he knew it would be either him or Julian.

Taking a deep breath, he ripped the bandage off. "A little over a year ago, my wife Katherine, our daughter Angela, and our unborn son, Joseph, died in a car crash. I was the only survivor."

"Oh my god, Marco." She went to get up, but he put his hand up to stop her.

"You rolled your car in the exact spot where they died. I wondered if it was Katherine who brought you here. Because what are the fucking odds that twenty years later, the girl I left behind shows up? I sat in your room night after night looking at you, with a million questions in my head. Why are you here? Why now? I thought that Julian finally figured out where I was and sent you to draw me out. But when Charlie showed me two sets of identification, I knew you were running. I am just having a very difficult time accepting the fact that you are here. I finally, after a year of surviving their deaths, laid them to rest in my mind. Then you show up. So, if I get angry or withdrawn, that would be why. It has nothing to do with what you say to me." She nodded at him. "I promised Katherine that I was going to help you, to free you from him so you can finally have the life you deserve. I feel responsible for what you have been through because I didn't take you with me. But I only had one set of papers, for me. So, we are in this together now, until the end. Beck, I will give my life to save you."

"Why would you do that?" she whispered.

"Because I have nothing to lose. My heart is broken, and if I hadn't promised Katherine a long time ago that I would go on living if anything ever happened to her, I would have joined them a long time ago."

"No." Her tears silently fell onto her cheeks.

Marco stood there looking at her. Just knowing the hell she had lived through, his heart was feeling something, and he wasn't sure he liked feeling anything other than total devastation. "I spent twenty years thinking about and grieving your death. Now that I know you didn't die that night, for kissing me, I'm not so sure I can survive it again."

Marco just stood there looking at her. "Beckett, Julian is going to come looking for you. Where did you get all that money?"

Her head snapped toward him. "You have the money? That sheriff told me the car burned. I need that money so I can get away."

"I have everything." He went to the kitchen and came back with the jar. "Including these."

"What are those?"

"Tracking devices. They were in your clothes and purse. There was one on the car as well, along with ten bricks of cocaine."

"What? Are you fucking kidding me?" She walked to the door, putting her boots on. "You have to give me the money. He knows where I am." He watched her freaking out. "Your father is dead now, so he will rape me. He hasn't touched me all this time because your father would have killed him. That's why I stabbed him. He was high and had every intention of taking me."

"He just woke up two days ago. We found the trackers the day after you crashed, so he isn't coming yet. Not yet. We have some time before he gets out of the hospital. That's why we are out here and not in town. Charlie had a bulletin come across his desk saying you are wanted for grand theft and suspicion of stabbing him. There was no photo, Beckett, so you are safe for now."

"As long as he is alive, I'll never be safe. I will kill myself before I let him touch me!" she shouted at him.

"And I promise you it will never happen. I'm not the scared boy I was twenty years ago."

"No, now you're a man with a death wish. I'm sorry, Marco, but I'm not going down like that. He won't kill me; he wants my virginity. God knows he's told me enough."

He wasn't sure he heard her right. "Beck, what are you saying? You're still a virgin?" She nodded slowly. "Jesus Christ." He was moving toward her. "Why?"

"Marco, I've loved you my whole life. It's always been you."

"I was dead, Beck."

In the smallest of voices, she said, "So was I."

He pulled her to his chest. "We need to stop him. He is coming for you, but he doesn't know I'm alive. Beck, we are going to need help."

She moved away from him. "Who is going to help us? No one will go against him."

"You did." He smiled. "Beckett, what do you know about what is happening there?"

She chuckled. "More than I should. Julian never cared what he said in front of me. He would tell his men that I was going to be his wife and wives weren't allowed to testify against their husbands."

"Why aren't you married yet?"

"Julian wanted to wait until your father died."

"I'm going to tell you something, and I don't want you to freak out." She looked at him. "The head of the organized crime unit for the F.B.I. is here. I want you to talk with him."

"No!" she shouted. "Julian has men in the F.B.I. If that man knows I'm here, Julian won't be far behind."

"Do you know the names of these men?"

"Yes, and cops and the elected officials who he owns."

"Fuck." He went to the kitchen and grabbed a piece of paper and a pen they had for Angela to draw. "I need you to write down their names and what they do."

When Beckett finished, she handed him the paper. Both sides were full. Looking at her, he agreed, "We need help. You said it yourself, if he finds you, you will kill yourself, and I'm already dead and don't really give a shit. So, I say we do this."

"You'll do this with me?"

"I owe you, Beck. I'll give you your freedom." She nodded. Pulling out his phone, he sent a text to Charlie. "We have about twenty-five minutes."

Marco watched Beckett stand by the window looking out. He couldn't imagine the abuse she had endured at the hands of his brother. She was still so tiny. Her height reached just below his shoulder, and she was rail thin. Thinner than Katherine was, but Katherine had a few inches on Beckett. "What's running through your head?"

She chuckled, not turning around. "The look on Julian's face when he realizes you're still alive."

"Who says he even needs to know?" But he had been thinking the same thing. He would love to see his face.

"Marco, I'm not so sure this is the best decision. You have a life here. Just give me the money and let me go. If he finds me, I will keep your secret."

"Beck, I abandoned you once, a long time ago. I knew then that I should have climbed that tree outside your window and took you with me. My mother gave her life to save me. I was scared and beaten, broken down by the years of abuse. There is no excuse for leaving you, but I'm not that scared little boy anymore."

"No, I don't suppose you are. But to give up this life you have made for yourself just to save me, Marco? I'm not worth it. Trust me. For twenty years, I have been struggling to stay alive, fighting him off. I have nothing. I am nothing. Julian made sure of that."

"Beck, you deserve to be free, to have a life of your own."

He watched her wipe a tear from her cheek. "To do what? To have what? He has hurt me so much over the years that it actually hurts sometimes to get out of bed. Hell, the majority of the time, I don't sleep for fear he is going to show up high or drunk to torture me."

He moved toward her, and she turned, tilting her head. Marco wrapped his hands around her head, his thumbs wiping away her tears. His voice was soft as he felt his heart warm. "I'm so sorry for leaving you."

It was the feeling of warmth that encased his soul when she wrapped her arms around his waist, which caused his breath to hitch in his chest. She felt like home. It was the car door that had his eyes opening. "Beck, I need you to go into the other room. I don't want this guy knowing you are here yet." She nodded, letting him go. He followed her to the door. "Go in the kitchen."

Opening the door, Charlie and Jay walked up. Jay greeted him, "Mr. Lucian."

"Miller, my name is Marc Miller."

"Sorry." Jay smiled as he moved into the house, taking off his boots and coat. The three of them moved into the living room, and Beckett moved to the wall outside it.

"What brings us here?"

Marco sat there looking at him for a long time. Jay's arrogance was pissing him off, and he was trying to rein in the overpowering desire he had to punch the man in the face. "Mr. Munch, your arrogance is going to be your downfall. No one is beyond reach where Julian Lucian is concerned."

"As I've said before, my department is tight."

Marco chuckled. "See? Arrogant. Well, how about I knock you down off that high fucking horse you've set yourself on?" Marco pulled the paper Beckett had written on out of his pocket and handed it to Jay. "I'm pretty sure you'll recognize more than a few names on that list. Your husband's name is on there. Those men and women are on Julian Lucian's payroll."

Marco watched as Jay read through the names. He watched him swallow hard, more than a few times. Looking at Jay, Marco saw the fear in the man's eyes. "How do you know this?"

"I just do."

"Why should I believe this?"

Beckett appeared in the doorway, "Because it's true."

All heads turned to her. "And who are you?" Jay said.

"My name is Beckett Angelo. I'm the one who stabbed Julian. My father was Marcel Lucian's right hand."

Marco looked at Jay; he wasn't breathing. He chuckled, shaking his head. "Breathe, Mr. Munch. Your horse seems to have slammed you to the ground."

"Are you kidding me?" Jay said softly. "How do I know you didn't make this up to save yourself from an attempted murder charge?"

Marco looked at Beckett, smiling. "Tell him, sweetheart."

She gave a small smile as she moved into the room, sitting on the couch next to Marco. "There are only a few people who know this about me, Mr. Munch, but I have an eidetic memory. It's bothersome the majority of the time, but I remember everything. What is on that paper is not only accurate but true. I don't know who you are, but Marco trusts you, or you wouldn't be here. I need to trust someone because Julian Lucian will come for me, and when he does, no one will be left standing. So, instead of threatening me with jail time for trying to kill the fucking bastard, who is the devil himself, help me send him back to hell."

Marco reached over and ran his hand down her back. "He'll help us. His husband's name is on that list. His ego is just a bit shaken right now."

Jay sat there looking at her. He was struggling with the nauseating excitement of finally having the ability to end the Lucian crime syndicate and the idea that he had Julian Lucian's attacker within his reach. "What's stopping me from arresting you and taking you back to Chicago?"

She laughed at him. "Your husband Christopher, well, he isn't gay. Hell, his name isn't even Christopher. It's Joey Malone."

"Fuck," Marco said under his breath. He knew Joey; maybe that's why he was staring at him the way he was.

"You might know him," she continued. "His street name is Slice, notorious for the way he kills people. No one has ever seen him, and you don't have any pictures of him, do you?" Jay swallowed hard. "Once a week, Tuesdays, he would come to the house to give his report to Marcel. Just curious, you never actually performed sex on him, did you? I know you didn't because Joey is a fucking perverse asshole. When he would have his women at the warehouse, it was always in the ass. I know because Julian would force me to watch. He would say that I needed to learn these things so I would know what was expected of me when we got married."

"I don't believe this, any of this!" Jay shouted, standing up. "I should just arrest you."

"Well, I can guarantee you that is not going to happen," she smart-mouthed him. "This man," she nodded her head toward Marco, "isn't going to let you."

Jay stood there with his nostrils flared.

"Calm down, Jay," Charlie said. "They are willing to help."

Jay grabbed the list and walked out. Marco chuckled when he heard the car door slam. "Charlie, I'm sorry about that. I didn't want Beckett to show herself yet. Is he going to be a problem or the solution?"

Charlie chuckled. "I'm sure he'll be fine. That was some potent information about his husband. It's not every day you find out that the man you love is a monster." He stood up. "Listen, keep her safe. I'll be back."

Marco looked at Beckett. "It's late. You should get some rest. How do you feel?"

She smiled. "I have a headache."

He went and got her something. "The spare room is the first door past the bathroom. I put your clothes in there. Fresh towels in the bathroom. Doc said to be careful of the stitches."

"Thank you."

He watched her walk out of the room. Marco locked the doors and shut off all the lights, then laid down on the couch.

Beckett softly closed the door before sliding down it, her hand covering her mouth as she quietly screamed. Her whole body shook as the memories of Marco flashed through her mind. He was alive. Her hand moved to the tattoo over her heart. She remembered the one and only kiss she shared with him. But now he had loved someone else. He was just as broken, if not more than she was. Beckett laid in bed with her clothes on and cried herself to sleep. But her dreams weren't dreams. They were nightmares.

The warmth of his hands as he caressed her chest, gently pinching her nipples. "Mmm... yes," she moaned. Her core heated up as the warmth of his hands moved down her body, removing her panties. Feather touches on her core. She opened her legs to welcome him.

The warmth of his body as he laid next to her, his fingers exploring her very personal place.

Beckett felt her back arch, lifting off the bed as he gently massaged her tight bundle of nerves. "Oh, yes," she moaned. His lips wrapped around her nipple as her orgasm ripped through her. His finger slipped inside of her, pumping deeper, making her come again. "Oh, God," she moaned softly, her body shaking.

Then it stopped. Everything stopped. The weight glided slowly across her chest, and then she felt the velvet softness on her lips. She slightly opened her mouth as he so sweetly pushed inside the warmth.

He felt so soft, yet hard as steel, slowly moving in and out, his moans soft as her tongue caressed him. "That's it. Out of all the blow jobs, your mouth is my favorite," he moaned as he slowly fucked her mouth.

The voice wasn't his. It wasn't her love's, but who's? She struggled to open her eyes, to pull herself out of the dream. Her hands pushed on his stomach, but he didn't move. His hips pushed harder. Then she felt his hand wrap around her hair, jerking her head back. His fingers dug into either side of her jaw, holding her mouth open while he pushed harder, deeper. Her screams were muffled by his cock as he came in her mouth, all over her face.

Beckett was gagging, trying to breathe, but her mouth and nose were filled with his release. When he finished, he climbed off her. Rolling off the bed onto the floor, she vomited, crying, screaming at him.

"I'll fucking kill you."

But Julian grabbed her by the hair, pulling her up. "That tight little pussy of yours is mine. You suck my cock like no other."

Beckett hit him while he laughed at her. "It was Marco in my dream. It will always be him!" she screamed at him.

Julian dropped her, landing a foot to her ribs, laughing.

〜

"Beckett," she heard in her head. She always heard his sweet voice after Julian hurt her. "Sweetheart." His hand touched her shoulder. He never touched her. Freaking out, Beckett pushed away.

"No!" she shouted. "No!"

"Beckett," the voice boomed. "Wake up, Beckett."

Her eyes flew open. It was hard to focus in the darkness. She realized she was fully clothed. "Hey," the voice said softly.

"Marco?" She was questioning herself.

"Yes, what happ—"

He didn't finish before Beckett flung herself at him, knocking him on his ass. Climbing on him, she wrapped herself around him like a monkey and burst into tears.

Marco lost his breath when she came into contact with him. It felt natural to wrap his arms around her. "Shh," he whispered in her neck. "What happened?"

She shook her head, pulling herself closer to him.

Marco held her until she calmed down. He slid his hands to her sides, his thumbs gently brushing the underside of her breasts, pulling her back. "What happened?" Their faces inches apart, he could feel her warm breath puffing gently on his lips.

She just sat there looking at him. Her fingers touched his lips, her eyes on his. "You're so beautiful."

He smiled. "Beckett." Her name came out in a strangled moan. She moved closer. "I can't," he got out just as her lips touched his. He felt his eyes close as her tongue barely touched his upper lip. She felt so good, and before he realized what he was doing, his hands were in her hair and he deepened the kiss. It was her moan that shocked him back to reality, pulling her away from him. "I can't do this." He moved away from her, got up, and walked out.

Marco pushed through the snow, tears running down his cheeks. "God, Kate, I'm so sorry. I can't do this to you." Clearing the bench, he sat down looking into the darkness. Nothing was making sense to him. He loved his wife; he shouldn't have felt the way he did when Beckett kissed him. It shook him to his core. It confused him by how right it felt, just like it did twenty years ago. "Aww, Kate, what am I going to do?"

She was fading from his memory, but his heart yearned to feel her. He knew it would never be again, and he knew it was time to let them go. Standing, he moved to the edge of the lake. "Kate, help me. Help me move forward. Is she my ever after?" He thought Katherine was his ever after. Turning, he looked at the cabin. No lights were on, just a faint glow from the fire.

It was the pull of the woman inside that unnerved him. "Is this how you move on?" he whispered to himself. Standing in the cold darkness of the night, Marco felt a warmth fill him from deep inside. Before his brain registered what his body was doing, he was moving toward the cabin. Opening the door, he didn't see Beckett anywhere, so he put more wood on the fire and laid on the couch. His mind swirled in a state of mass confusion.

He knew what he felt when he kissed Beckett; he knew because, for years after he left, he felt it. He felt her, but eventually, it faded. All the memories of that life faded as he became Marc Miller. She faded, and when he met Katherine, it all disappeared. Now, here she was twenty years later, and everything he felt that fated night was back. The way her lips felt on his, the way she tasted, so sweet. He lay there with his arm across his face trying to shut his mind off when her voice broke the silence.

"I was dreaming, well, having a nightmare." He removed his arm to see her small silhouette in the doorway. "Julian did horrible things to me while I slept, but my dreams were always about you, about us. He knew it, and he would use my aroused state to touch me, to do things to me. I would wake up from his moans as he shoved his cock in my mouth. He would pop my jaw so I couldn't bite him."

"Beck, I'm so sorry." His voice cracked as he held back his tears.

"I don't think I've really slept since I turned twenty-one. That's when it all started. Marco, I'm sorry for kissing you. I shouldn't have done that. It's just... well, it's the first time I've ever felt safe."

He put his hand out. "Come here, Beck. Come here, I'll hold you while you sleep." She moved toward him. Her hand slipped into his. "I won't let him hurt you again," he said softly as he gently pulled her down on the couch. He tucked her between him and the back of the couch, his arms wrapping around her. "I've got you, sweetheart. You sleep."

Beckett was still shaking. Marco wondered if she was cold. He hadn't started the little stove in the bedroom. Reaching up, he pulled the blanket off the back of the couch and covered them both. She tucked her head under his chin and wrapped her arm around his waist.

Taking a deep breath, he let the worry go, closed his eyes, and let sleep take him.

Marco's eyes opened to the sound of his phone vibrating on the table. Picking it up, he saw it was Charlie. Smiling at the warmth that surrounded him, he put the phone down, pulling Beckett closer to him.

"Mmm…" she moaned, pulling him tighter. "Thank you."

He chuckled. "I don't think I've slept this good in over a year."

She giggled. "I know I haven't ever slept like this." Then she pulled back to look at him. "You aren't that skinny boy I once knew."

Marco laughed, his hand moving the strange red hair off her face. "No, sweetheart, I'm far from it." His fingers slid into her hair. He wanted to kiss her again, but he just looked into her eyes, into her shattered soul. "Aww, Beck, I'm so sorry for the things he did to you."

He watched her fight back her tears. "In the end, it doesn't matter. None of it does because it brought me here," her voice softened as the tears fell from her eyes, "to you."

His thumb ran across her bottom lip. Her eyes closed as more tears fell. Marco felt his head move, his eyes closing as his lips gently touched hers. His phone vibrated on the table again, causing both of them to giggle. Marco let her go, untangling himself from her to pick up the phone. "Yeah?"

"Jesus, I've been calling you for the past hour."

"I was sleeping, Charlie. What's going on?"

"Let's just say you need to get back here. We need to talk. Come the back way."

"No shit."

"You've got the CAT?"

Marco hung up. "Beck, we need to go. Get all your things, leave nothing behind. No trace."

She was off the couch and moving. Marco stood at the back door waiting for her. When she walked in, he handed her gloves and a hat. "Listen, when we walk out this door, I need you to listen to me. No smart mouth. You do as I say, okay?" Beckett nodded. She was scared shitless. "I'm going to throw you over my shoulder." He handed her a broom. "It's snowing out, but I need you to cover my footprints the best you can."

They worked their way into the woods, to the barn. Marco put her down. "You all right?"

She was a bit dizzy, but she smiled. "Why did you carry me?"

"One set of footprints." He unlocked the barn door so she could go in. Marco used the broom to cover their footprints.

"Where are we?"

"The barn. Charlie and I built this about fifteen years or so ago." He chuckled. "Katherine didn't even know it was here. It's about a mile from the cabin."

"You own this?"

Marco smiled. "About twenty-five hundred acres."

"Marco, why do you own this?"

He was working to uncover the CAT. "Well, it was the cabin first. It's where I lived for a long time. Then, over the years, the people who owned the land surrounding the cabin started to pass away, so I bought up their land."

"Can I ask what you do for a living?"

"I own a local construction company with a buddy of mine." He grabbed the gas cans, putting them in the back of the CAT.

"Marco, why do you have this thing?"

He opened the door for her and helped her up, then he opened the back doors of the barn. Once outside, he closed the doors, and they began the long journey back to town.

"It was always for this, in case Julian ever came looking for me. But when I met Katherine, we bought the cottage, and I really didn't need it anymore. I just never got around to selling it. Then when Angela was born and we started spending Christmases up here, I was glad that I didn't get rid of it."

"You lived in fear, didn't you?" She was sad for him.

"I did, for a long time. But as I grew into my body and became this man, my fears lessened. Now, I'm afraid for you, not for me."

"He won't kill me." Her voice cracked.

"I'm not willing to take that chance. Beck, I can say this over and over again, but I'm so sorry for leaving you behind. The guilt nearly killed me."

"I understand why you did. I was your friend back then. I knew what Julian and your father did to you. I didn't blame you. I'm just glad you aren't dead. What he did to you that night has haunted me for twenty years. He taunted me, telling me that would happen to any boy or man who touched me. Funny how I used that against him in the end."

"What do you mean?"

"He was high, I mean really high. His goon squad came to get me, and I fought back. I knew what he was going to do. Well, one of them knocked me out. When I woke up, the guy who hit me was duct-taped to a chair. Julian was jacked on coke, so I insinuated they might have molested me." Marco chuckled, and Beckett laughed. "He went bat shit crazy and killed all three of them. That's when I knew he was going to rape me. He had nothing to lose, so I grabbed the knife and stabbed him."

"Beck, you stabbed him sixteen times."

She giggled, just like she did when they were kids. Marco felt it all the way to his core. He knew he would die protecting her.

"He deserved that and more. I thought about cutting his dick off, but that meant I would have had to touch him; besides, he was dead already." She got quiet. "But he isn't."

He reached over and squeezed her leg. "We will beat him. You will be free."

When she exploded in her defiance, his heart warmed. It was one of the things he loved about her when they were kids. She was so tiny, but she always acted like she was a giant.

"Really? We are in the middle of the wilderness in a giant machine, hiding."

"Not hiding."

"Then what, Marco? What are we doing? We're running from the fucking big bad wolf, who is going to kill us both. We can't win. It's not the same as it was twenty years ago. Marco, they will die for him. They are terrified of being tortured by that sadistic motherfucker."

"Beckett!" he yelled, laughing.

"What?"

"Sweetheart, fear can be a very powerful motivator."

"Great! Marco, just give me the money and my papers so I can disappear. You don't care if you die, but I do."

"I might have changed my mind," he mumbled more to himself than to her, thinking about Katherine. He knew she was gone, and Beckett was the first girl who made him feel like life was worth it. He had always planned on going back for her, but the more years that passed, the more he put them away as childish dreams. Then he met Katherine, and nothing mattered to him but her. She stole his heart with her bright spirit and wild personality. Neither of them said anything for a long time. When Marco stopped the CAT and shut it off, he turned to look at Beckett. "When I left all those years ago, I left with a broken spirit, a broken heart, and a broken body. Beck, I was coming back for you. But the years got away from me. Then I met Katherine. She was so much like you. She stole my heart, and everything else was forgotten until last week. When I pulled you out of that car, when your head fell back and this strange red hair fell from your face, my heart stopped. It was like my brain froze. The freckles that run across your cheeks felt so familiar to me. Then when Charlie laid your license on my counter, I nearly passed out. Every promise I made to myself came flooding back. Every moment we shared that I thought I had forgotten came back. That kiss we shared, the one that changed me was right there in front of me. Don't get me wrong, Beck, I love my wife to the depth of my very being. But now, what I felt for you all those years ago is in there, too, and it's tearing me up."

She didn't say anything for a long time, her eyes focused on her hands. "I've loved you my whole life, Marco. Remember when you helped me with that project for school and we did all that research about the sugar skills?"

He chuckled. Pulling off his glove, he pushed up his coat sleeve to show her the two tattoos on his wrist. "One for my mom and one for Marco Lucian."

Her eyes stared at his arm. Pulling off her gloves, she unzipped her coat and turned in her seat to face him.

Marco watched as she slowly unbuttoned her blouse. She moved the material to show him the exact same sugar skull tattooed over her left breast. "For the only boy I ever loved, Marco Lucian."

He couldn't look away; the detail was incredible. His eyes moved to hers. He had no clue he moved until Beckett was in his arms, straddling him. His kiss was fierce at first, and she gave as good as she got. Marco slowed it down because she had been manhandled enough. When he tasted salt, he pulled back and looked at her, seeing tears streaming down her cheeks.

"Sweetheart," his thumbs wiped her tears, "what is going on in that head of yours?"

"I've dreamt of this my whole life. You riding in on your white horse to scoop me up and take me away. That kiss kept my heart beating. I wanted to do a Romeo and Juliet, but Julian wouldn't let me out of his sight for that first year.

"Beck," he whispered, pulling her toward him. Gently, he kissed her.

Pulling back, she touched his lips. "Please, Marco, don't do this. Don't give me hope. I've loved you my whole life. I can't..."

He ran his thumb along her lips, his eyes searching hers. "Beck, you have been in my heart for most of my life. I'm at fault for burying it. I'm not playing with you. I'm so sorry for not coming back. But I'm here now, and I will stand with you until the end." He wiped her tears. "I'm not that scared, scrawny boy anymore."

Her eyes moved to his chest as she gently touched him. Marco closed his eyes. "No, I don't suppose you are." Her warm breath fanned his lips. "Marco, I am so glad you survived." She pressed her lips against his.

Marco got lost in the kiss, the warmth filling his entire being. Pulling back, he put his forehead on hers. "Beckett," his voice sounded strangled.

"I know. I'm sorry." She went to move, but he held her in place.

"No, sweetheart." He smiled at the look on her face. "I... I... Aww, hell." His mouth covered hers. She was working him up, bringing a sense of life back into his soul. He felt himself wanting to let go, to fold to the desire she was bringing out in him.

Beckett pulled back. "Marco." His name a whisper on his lips.

"Yeah, I know what you mean. We need to stop. Charlie will be here soon. We need to go."

Smiling, she shook her head, wrapping her arms around his neck. "Hold me," she breathed on his neck.

He slid his hands up the back of her jacket, his fingers coming to rest on the sides of her breasts. They sat like that until Charlie walked up and knocked on the door of the CAT. Beckett got back in her seat while Marco helped Charlie up.

"We've got a problem." He smiled at Marco, nodding his head. "A big fancy lawyer showed up to get Christopher released."

"Anthony Jones?" Beckett asked Charlie, who nodded. "That's Julian's lawyer. He knows I'm here."

"I don't think he does." Charlie sounded convinced.

Marco looked at Charlie. "How did he know where he was? Only you, me, and Jay knew."

"No, Alex and Maggie as well."

"Charlie, how long have they been with you?"

"Maggie, maybe thirty years. Alex..." He sat there looking at Marco.

"What?" Beckett sat up straight.

"He's known all along where I've been. How the fuck did he find me?"

"I don't think it was Julian. I think it was your father," Charlie said. "Now that your father is gone, Julian would have this knowledge."

Beckett shook her head. "No, he wouldn't. Marcel kept a great many secrets. Not to mention, Julian is a drug addict."

"How can you be sure?" Charlie questioned her.

She laughed. "Julian has been doing drugs for the last five years. He's been trying to get Marcel into the drug trade, but Marcel, as evil as he was, refused to deal in drugs and flesh. I don't have proof, but I wouldn't be surprised if he didn't have a hand in Marcel's death."

Marco looked at Charlie. "Does Alex know about Beckett?"

"No one except for Jay knows about her."

"Where is Jay?"

"He took your list and headed back to Chicago."

"Does he know about the lawyer?"

"Yeah, I called him."

"Excuse me," Beckett said. "Is this 'Christopher,'" she air-quoted, "Joey still in jail?"

"Yep."

"Can Alex let him out?"

"Nope, but I can only hold him for ninety-six hours at the most, so you've got two days."

"Can you find out if Julian is still in the hospital?" Marco looked at Beckett.

"From what Jay said before he left, he's in pretty bad shape. He's going through withdrawals. His body isn't handling anything very well." He looked at Beckett. "You might be looking at a murder charge."

She didn't say anything.

"Marco, Christopher knows about the cabin. Why don't you leave the CAT here and let me take the two of you back to the cottage?"

Marco sat there for a long time, thinking. "Charlie, can I use your phone?" Charlie handed it to him, and he got out of the CAT, walking away so they couldn't hear him. He scrolled through the numbers until he came to the one he wanted. "Hey, it's Marc Miller."

"Mr. Miller, what can I do for you?"

He chuckled. "You can figure out a way to get me in to see my brother. If he's in that bad of shape, I'd like him to know I'm still alive."

"I can't do that."

"Why not? Can't you just go see him, and I can tag along? Pretend I'm an agent as well. I do own one of those nifty suits you guys wear, and I even have the fancy sunglasses."

Jay laughed. "I was actually getting things together to come back there."

"Well, I'll jump on a plane and see you in, what, five hours?"

"Let me know when and where and I'll pick you up."

"Thanks, Jay." Marco got back in the CAT. "Charlie, can Beckett stay with you? I have something I need to do. I'll pick her up when I'm done." He nodded. Looking at Beckett, he told her, "You go with Charlie. His wife Elizabeth will love you. They are the people who took care of me when I turned up here twenty years ago. I'm going back to the cabin to get my truck, but I'll see you in a few hours."

"But…" she said.

"Trust me. Trust Charlie. He won't let anything happen to you."

CHAPTER SEVEN

Jay met Marco at the gate and escorted him to the hospital. "Now, when we get up there, don't say a word to anyone. Let me do the talking."

"That's fine. Is his room wired?"

"No, but he has security around the clock. I don't have any credentials for you, so hopefully, mine will get us both in."

Marco laughed. "You're head of your division. Why would they question you?"

"Maybe because we have the head of the Lucian crime family in a hospital room. This is bigger than you know, Marco. The families are running scared. There is word of infighting concerning who is going to take over when or if Julian dies."

Smiling, he said, "Well, it would by rights be me. But they don't need to know that. As far as the families are concerned, my big brother killed me twenty years ago."

Walking down the hall to the ICU, Marco felt a twinge of excitement at seeing his brother's face when telling him who he is. Jay was talking to the two guards outside his room; it took more than a few minutes of talking and several phone calls for them to gain access to the room. Marco wasn't expecting the wave of emotions to flood his body the way they did when he saw his brother. It was rage mostly, anger, hatred.

Jay walked up to the bed. "Well, Julian, looks like you got yourself into some kind of predicament."

Julian had a strangled chuckle. "Don't worry about me, Munch. I've got it covered."

Jay laughed. "Yes, I can see that. So, who did you piss off this time? Whoever it was sure did a number on you."

"You know damn well who did this to me, and that little bitch is going to pay for it."

"I don't think so," Marco said.

Julian started coughing when he laughed. "I'll make sure of it, and you won't be able to do a damn thing about it."

Marco moved closer to Julian. "I'm sorry, brother, but I am going to do something about it. Beckett is with me, and you will never get your hands on her."

Julian just sat there looking at Marco. Then he smiled. "You aren't my brother. Both of those fuckers are dead."

"Wrong again. I just wanted to see you, to let you know that I am still alive and living a good life. Beckett is going to be free of you." Julian looked at him for a long time. "You see, brother, all I have to do is go to the family and tell them I'm alive, and then I'll be the boss. And if you survive this," Marco leaned in so he could look into his eyes, "they will never find your body. You have hurt her for the last time. You will never see her again." Marco saw the truth in his eyes. He knew Julian knew it was him. "No one told you, did they? No one knows, Julian. I work for the F.B.I., and no one knows, so all your paid hands are all going down right along with you. I just wanted to see your fucking face when you realized that I am still alive. You have a good time here, and I hope you recover because I am going to find the greatest of pleasures breaking your fucking neck."

Julian looked at Munch. "You heard him threaten me."

Munch laughed. "I didn't hear a thing. The machines were making too much noise."

Marco chuckled and walked out of the room. He thought he would find some satisfaction in seeing Julian. In letting him know he was still alive. But he found himself feeling sorry for him. He looked like shit, frail, sick. Marco didn't know any drug addicts, so he wasn't sure if that's what one looked like. When they were in the elevator, Marco looked at Jay. "Is that what a drug addict looks like? He's skin and bones."

"I'm afraid it is. Marco, your brother is in bad shape. He's detoxing, and his body is trying to heal. There is a great chance that he isn't going to make it."

"Good, then I won't have to worry about killing the bastard."

"No, but Miss Angelo will be facing a murder charge."

Marco laughed. "No, she won't. But I need to get back. You know where to find me. Oh, and thanks for this. Now, I need to get the hell out of this city."

Marco grabbed a cab back to the airport. By the time he returned to his cottage, it was the middle of the night. He texted Charlie that he was home and asked if Beckett was sleeping.

Ten minutes later, there was a knock on the door. When he opened the door, she was standing there. Instinctively, he reached out, pulling her to his chest. Charlie stood behind her with a small smile on his face. Marco nodded to him, and they went inside. "Come on, sweetheart. You need to get some sleep."

She nodded into his chest, and he led her to his new room. "Marco, I can't sleep in the same bed you shared with your wife."

He touched her face. "I didn't share this room with Katherine or that bed. It's all brand new. To be honest, Beck, I haven't slept in a bed in over a year. Our room was upstairs."

She stood there looking at him. "I'm so sorry for everything that has happened to you."

"Thank you, but it's over now. I've struggled for a long time with letting them go. I guess I'm still struggling, but it's getting easier." His voice was soft. "Go on, get some sleep. I'll be right out there on the couch."

Beckett nodded, moving away from him. Marco gently shut the door, not sure he wanted to be away from her, but there was no other choice right now. Julian knew he was alive and that Beckett was with him. Hell was coming in one form or another. He needed to stay alert, and not full of emotions he was having for her.

Marco lay on the couch thinking about the woman in the other room, in his room, in his bed. His eyes grew heavier with each blink of his eyes. Sleep finally won over, taking him down the rabbit hole.

"Marco," the voice was faint. "Come on, baby. Wake up."

His smile was automatic. He knew that voice, his beautiful Katherine. Opening his eyes, he saw her smiling at him. "What's the matter, baby?"

She reached out to touch his face. "It's time, my love."

"Time for what? Is the baby coming?" His heart felt full at seeing her sparkling eyes.

Smiling, she shook her head and giggled. "No, silly, Joseph is here with me. It's time, baby, for you to let us go. We will always be here." He felt the warmth on his chest as she touched his heart.

"I can't. I don't want you to be gone. I love you, Kate, so much." He felt the tears come.

"I know, and I love you. But it's time to let us go. It's time for you to move on. It's why we left you. I know now that your heart was not mine to take. I know you gave it to me; I feel your love, Marco."

"No, Kate, it was yours to take."

She smiled at him, then leaning down, she gently kissed him. "I love you, husband. It's time. Go keep your promise to me. Go love again, live."

He watched her move away from him. "Kate."

She smiled and waved as she faded from his dream.

Marco's eyes flew open. Sitting up, he searched the room for her. Touching his lips, he smiled. "I'll always love you, wife," he whispered. Pushing up, he got a drink and used the bathroom.

Standing in the doorway, he looked at the living room. She was gone, giving him her blessing to move on. His eyes moved to the bedroom door. Quietly, he opened it to check on Beckett. He wasn't prepared for what he saw. She was lying on her stomach completely naked, the blanket barely covering her ass.

It wasn't his intention to walk into the room, but he found himself standing next to the bed. Her arm moved, reaching for the blanket. She pulled it up and under her chest to snuggle. He couldn't help but wonder if she was his future. What kind of future could they have if Julian survived? If he died, would she be charged with murder? He moved to leave. "Marco?" she whispered.

"I was just checking on you. Go back to sleep."

"You all right?"

He heard the blankets as she sat up. "Just a dream. I'm fine." He turned to close the door. She was sitting with the blanket around her.

"You want to talk about it?"

He stood there looking at her. "No, it's fine. I'm fine. Go back to sleep. You need your rest." He pulled the door almost closed.

"Marco, don't." Her voice came out barely a whisper.

His eyes closed. He knew if he stayed, he was going to kiss her, touch her. He couldn't do that to her. "Beck..."

"No, don't make an excuse. Stay with me. I need to feel safe. With what's coming..." she stopped.

Marco heard her sniffle. He let go of the door. She was in his arms trembling. "I got you. Come here." He pulled her into his hold as he laid down. Her breath was warm on his neck. "Aww, Beck," he moaned.

He felt her smile. "I know," she whispered, her lips moving on the flesh of his neck. "Kiss me," she moaned.

Turning his head to her, his lips found hers in the dark. Shifting his body, changing their embrace, he held her face and got lost in her. Lost in the gentle rhythm of the gentleness of her lips. "Beckett," he whispered, pulling back to look at her. "Let's get some sleep."

Her smile nearly did him in as she cuddled up to him. He knew he should tell her where he went. But he decided it didn't matter anymore. The only thing that mattered was keeping her safe and giving her, her freedom.

~

Marco woke in the early hours of the morning. A strange feeling washed over him. It felt like someone walked over his grave. He was careful getting up. Gently, he closed the door behind him, then went looking for his phone. Swiping it on, he saw a message from Charlie.

'Call me'

Looking at the time stamp, it said 5:30 in the morning. He dialed Charlie. "Hey, what's going on?"

"Marco, Julian didn't make it."

He spun around, looking at the bedroom door. "Fuck. Where is Jay?"

"He should be here in a few hours. Christopher is still in jail. I'll meet you up at the cabin."

"You got it." He disconnected the call and went to wake up Beckett. "Sweetheart, come on, we need to go."

She sat up, the blanket falling away from her. Marco froze, his eyes moving down to her chest unintentionally. Slowly, he turned his head. *She's fucking perfect.* "Get dressed. We need to go." He turned and walked out of the room. "Jesus," he whispered, running his hand across his head. Looking at the door, he felt his insides stir. He hadn't felt like this in a long time. He didn't think he would ever feel this way again.

He was quick opening the door. She had her back to him and was pulling up her jeans. Beckett turned as she buttoned the top button, just as his hands wrapped around her head, his mouth covering hers. Marco picked her up, her legs wrapped around him and he sat on the edge of the bed. Pulling back, his thumb ran across her lips. His eyes moved down her body. Her nipples were hard, her breasts perfect, and he was a man who had felt dead for so long. She was waking him up. It wasn't what he intended to do; she could be going to prison, but his hands left her face. One wrapped around her waist, the fingers of his other gently brushed her nipple. When he looked at her, she had her lip pulled between her teeth, her eyes closed. "Aww, Beck," he moaned.

Her eyes slowly opened. Leaning forward to kiss him, her breast pressing into his hand, he cupped it. She barely fit. Squeezing it, he ran his thumb along her nipple. Her moan vibrated on his lips, her breath pushing against his.

"We need to go, sweetheart."

Nodding her head, she got off his lap and watched him walk out of the room.

Marco adjusted himself in his jeans; he hadn't had an erection in a very long time.

"Holy shit," Beckett whispered. He felt like she always imagined he would. She quickly finished getting dressed. Marco was leaning against the counter when she walked into the kitchen. She stood there looking at him. His eyes were nearly black. "I should apologize for that, but I won't because I'm not sorry. Beck…"

She stopped him. "Don't. I'm not stupid, Marco. I know you love your wife, and I think I know that you haven't been with anyone since her. But you have always been my heart. What happened in there, whatever might happen between us is what I've dreamt of my whole life. So, don't feel like you are hurting me or are going to hurt me when this is over and we part ways. I'm fine with it." She was trying to be brave for him, but she wasn't fine with having bits of him because she wanted all of him forever.

He was fast, startling her when he picked her up, sitting her on the island. He kissed her hard. "Beck, it's not like that."

"It doesn't matter right now. We have a war to fight. I thought we needed to go."

He smiled at her, that same smile she remembered. "You're right, we need to go." Helping her down, they gathered their gear and left. Nothing was said on the trip back to the cabin. When they went in,

Marco started a fire. "I need to get some more wood. I'll be back in a few." He kissed her on the forehead.

Beckett made her way to the kitchen, the smile still on her face, her core still vibrating, her panties still wet. She made coffee and then breakfast for them. Marco came back into a house filled with the smell of breakfast. Dropping the wood, he turned to find Beckett leaning against the door frame.

"Are we going to talk about what happened?"

He chuckled as he approached her, his knuckles brushing along her jaw. Tilting her head up, he kissed her. "Nope. You taste like coffee."

"I made us breakfast. You hungry?"

"I am, but I don't think food is going to settle this hunger growing inside of me."

Her eyes got huge. "Oh."

He laughed, moving past her on his way to the bathroom. Tucking her lip in, she watched him walk away. "Damn."

After they ate and Marco cleaned up, they sat in the living room, Beckett on the couch, Marco on the chair. "What's wrong?" She could feel the tension.

"A great many things. In all the conversations we've had, not once have you mentioned Benny. Why is that?" He watched her eyes as they filled with tears.

"He died five years ago in a car accident. Shortly after that, your father's health started to decline."

"Did Julian kill him?"

"I think so, but he never said anything. But it was right around the time he started doing drugs and tried to get your father into dealing. Marcel and Julian would have some huge fights about it."

"Do you think Julian murdered my father?"

"I wouldn't put it past him. Your father had a secret safe that is one of those biometric ones. I'm not sure, but I think it needs like blood or DNA to open it."

"Does Julian know about it?"

"I'm not sure."

"How do you know?"

"I heard my mom and dad talking about it one night."

Marco nodded. "Beck, are there people who witnessed the abuse he inflicted on you? People who would go against Julian?"

She sat there looking at him, not saying anything. She got up and stood by the window, looking out at the snow falling.

"Beck?"

"He's dead, isn't he? We're back here because he's dead." Marco stood. "No, don't. This morning, what we did, it was because you found out he died." Her tears fell. "Wasn't it?! You are no different than him, only you use kindness instead of evil. Just give me the money and my papers and let me go, because I'm so tired of the fucking Lucian brothers. You are both cut from the same cloth."

He stood there smiling. Every neuron in his body was alive listening to her slam him. "You haven't changed one bit. Well, no, that's not true. You've matured into an incredible woman. A sexy as hell woman. A woman I want to get to know again." He stepped forward. "So, no, I am nothing like Julian because I will never hurt you like that, and no, Marco Lucian died twenty years ago. Hi, my name is Marc Miller." He put his hand out, and Beckett put her hand out to shake his. Pulling her to him, he whispered on her lips, "And no, I'm not giving you the money or the papers because I don't want you to leave." He kissed her.

When she pushed on his chest, he let her go. "No. Don't. I can't do this. I don't want this. Either you give me the money and help me get out of here, or I'm going to prison for killing him."

"No, you're not. I won't let that happen. I promised you I would give you your freedom and I will."

"Don't make promises you can't keep," she shouted. "I'm tired of broken promises, broken dreams. That fucker took everything from me. I should have been your wife. I should have been your first."

He didn't mean to laugh, but he did. "Sweetheart, Jenny McMann was my first. Sophomore year."

"What? Ewe, seriously? She was such a slut."

"I know." He smiled.

"That's disgusting."

"Hey, I was sixteen, my cock was hard all the time. It's a boy thing. I needed to do something with it because, trust me, fisting it in the shower wasn't cutting it."

She stuck her fingers in her ears. "I don't need to know this! You're disgusting. La-la-la-la-la," she yelled as she left the room.

Marco watched her with a huge smile on his face. But that smile faded as he heard multiple doors slam. Snapping his head to look out the window, he saw Charlie, Jay, and two other men standing in the drive and walking toward the cabin. "Fuck." He knew he wasn't going to let them take her, and he was pretty sure Charlie wouldn't have brought them there if that was their plan.

Marco opened the door. "Gentlemen." Charlie walked in and patted him on the shoulder, giving him a small smile. Marco relaxed a bit. "Would you mind taking off your shoes?"

Once in the living room, Jay started the conversation. "Mr. Miller, this is the Director of the division I work for, Allen Brick, and his Deputy Director, John Adams. Gentlemen, this is Marc Miller." Marco shook hands with the men, and they all sat down. "I took your list and had a discussion with these men. We all agree that it's a pretty damning list."

"We've started an investigation," Mr. Brick said. "We would like to talk to you about a few things."

"Well, Mr. Brick, I'm not sure what you think I might know."

"Mr. Munch led me to believe you are, in fact, Marco Lucian."

Marco laughed. "Mr. Brick, Marco Lucian was murdered by his older brother twenty years ago."

"But the body was never found."

"That's irrelevant."

"We need your help."

"I'm sorry, Mr. Brick, but I can't help you."

The two men sat there looking at one another for a long time. "Julian Lucian died last night; you have nothing to fear."

Marco leaned forward, resting his arms on his legs. "Julian Lucian has not been a fear that I've entertained for a very long time. His death means nothing to me. But it should mean something to you. It should mean the end of the Lucian family."

"It's not as easy as that. Word around is that the heads of the corresponding families want justice. There is a move for control within the family."

"It means nothing to me."

"No, perhaps not, but it may mean something to the person who ended him."

"Is that a threat, Mr. Brick?"

"Just an observation, Mr. Miller. Just an observation."

Marco shifted his eyes to Jay. "So, you got knocked off your horse two times in one day, and you run crying to your boss?"

"We are here to help," Jay said.

"Is that what you call this?" He looked at Brick. "Let me guess how you want to help. In exchange for ending the bastard that killed Marco Lucian, Benny Lucian, and Marcel Lucian, you want me to rise from the fucking dead and take control of the family? Be your snitch?"

"Well, we would need to work out the details, but yes."

Beckett stepped into the room, her eyes on Marco. "Not in a million fucking years is that going to happen." She looked at Brick. "My name is Beckett Angelo. I stabbed Julian Lucian sixteen times." Then she looked at Marco, who was now standing. "You will not sell your soul to Satan to save me. I won't let you."

"Please come and join us, Miss Angelo. I understand you are the author of this list."

"No!" Marco was moving toward her. "No, Beck."

"You have a life. I have nothing. In the end, I'm a murderer just like Julian." Looking at Brick, she told him, "I know more than you think I know."

"You are not doing this," Marco growled at her.

Her eyes were on Brick. "Mr. Miller lost his family in an accident last year. He has a death wish. He will not survive this. I can and will, in exchange for some leniency in my sentencing."

Marco grabbed her arm, pulling her into the hall. "Stop it, Beck. This isn't going to happen."

She moved around him to talk to Brick. "I have an eidetic memory."

Marco picked her up and carried her to the bedroom. Kicking the door shut, he spun around, pressing her against the door. "No, Beck. Don't do this."

She touched his face. "You are alive, which is all I ever wanted. I can't let you do this to save me. They will kill you, and I can't survive that again."

He shook his head. "No, Beck. I just got you back."

She giggled. "You've had a whole life here without me. You knew where I was. I've been fighting this life for twenty years. I'm tired of it. I'm so tired of being Beckett Angelo, oldest daughter of Anthony Angelo. Killing Julian was the only way to save myself from him. Now, I'll do this to save myself from them. I don't need you to save me, Marco." Her voice softened as she wiped the tear off his cheek. "I don't."

His kiss was fierce, but she gave as good as she got. Pulling back, she looked at him. "You've been safe for twenty years, so let me keep you safe," she whispered.

"No, Beck. If I have to lock you up, I will. You are not going back there."

"Who said I was going back there?" She tapped her head. "What I have in here is more than enough. Let me go, Marco."

"No. You are here with me now. I don't want you to go." His fear was very real to him.

"Please put me down. However this plays out, we are going to leave each other, either by death or by jail. This isn't our ever after." She felt the tears coming, and her voice cracked. "You replaced me once, and you can replace me again." Marco shook his head. "For twenty years, I dreamt of you, of this. In my heart, I knew it would never happen, but it was still my dream." She kissed him. "Thank you for giving me this dream. Put me down, Marco."

He dropped his head to her chest. "I can't. I can't let you do this. I'm so sorry for not coming back for you."

Her hands held his head, her lips gently kissing it. "It's the way it was supposed to be." She felt his hands loosen on her thighs. Slowly, he let her slide down the door. Beckett put her hands on his chest, and he stepped back. Touching his lips, she whispered, "I will always love you."

He just stood there looking at her as she opened the door and walked out.

Beckett walked into the living room, taking the seat Marco had been sitting in. "I have a few questions. If I do this, Mr. Miller is not to be involved. He has suffered enough," she turned her head to look at Marco, who was leaning against the door frame, "with the loss of his family last year."

"Deal," Brick said.

Looking back at Brick she asked, "Do you have Malone, the deputy and the lawyer in custody?"

"Yes, but who is Malone?"

"His husband," she nodded to Jay, "is Joey Malone."

Brick snapped his head toward Jay. "Are you kidding?"

"I had no idea who he was," Jay defended.

"Mr. Brick," Beckett said, "I need to talk to all three of them, separately. Alone."

"Can I ask why?"

"Well, the deputy was placed here for a reason. I want to know why. The lawyer was Marcel's lawyer, not Julian's. He has information, and he won't talk to you. Joey, well, I have a few things to say to him. After I talk to them, I will tell you everything I know."

Brick sat there looking at her. "You have a deal. The transport trucks will be on the highway. I'll have them pull over and we can go."

Beckett got up, walking past Marco. He reached out, pulling her into his chest. "Don't do this. Don't expose yourself like this."

"I won't let you die again," she whispered. "This is the world I live in. It's the world I need to end. You are free," she put her hand on his chest, "and I need you to stay free." Becket pulled away from him.

One by one, they all walked past him; Charlie was the last. "I'll make sure she comes back. Good to see that spark back."

Marco looked at him. "I'm going with you. I don't trust them." Charlie nodded.

CHAPTER EIGHT

As they drove up the highway, Marco could see three black semi-trailers pulled over on the side of the road. Marco got out when Charlie stopped, moved to the car in front of them, opened the door, and pulled Beckett out. "You don't have to do this," he whispered into her neck as he held her.

"I couldn't save you twenty years ago because I was a child. Now, I'm armed and I will keep you safe."

"Aww, Beck, I can do this."

She stepped back. "No, I've got this." Turning away from him, she said to Brick, "I want to talk to the deputy first." He nodded, heading to the middle truck. Everyone followed. Reaching for the door, Beckett said, "Alone. Have everyone leave. I know it's all recorded, so alone."

Brick opened the door. "Let's clear the truck. Everyone out."

When the truck was empty, Beckett climbed inside, and Brick shut the door behind her. Grabbing a chair, she moved it to the box Alex was in."

"Do you know who I am?"

"No."

"Why are you here?"

"No one told me. Five men walked into the office, handcuffed me, and now I'm here."

She smiled at him. "Not here in this truck, but here in this town."

"I live here."

"But you didn't until twenty years ago. Before that, you lived in Chicago."

"How do you know that?"

"My name is Beckett Angelo." She watched his reaction. He swallowed hard. "Marcel Lucian is dead. Now, the next questions I'm going to ask you, depending on how you answer will determine how your future looks. Do you now work for Julian Lucian?"

"No."

"Why are you here?"

"Mr. Lucian hired me to watch out for his youngest son Marco."

"Julian murdered Marco twenty years ago. I know because I was there."

"No, he didn't. Mr. Lucian and his wife saved him. Got him out. I was hired to follow him and to watch out for him."

"So, Marcel knew his son was alive?"

"Yes."

"Why did you call that lawyer?"

"He was my contact. When Munch showed up and they arrested that guy, I thought it was strange, so I called Mr. Jones. He showed up a few days later. But Charlie wouldn't release the guy."

"How often did you report to Mr. Jones?"

"Once a month."

"So, Marcel knew all about Marco's life? That he was married, had children, the accident?"

"Yes."

Beckett stood, her mind going a hundred miles a second. "Thank you," she said as she walked away. When she got out of the truck, she looked at Brick. "The lawyer next."

Marco just looked at her. When their eyes locked, she gave him a tight smile. Brick led them all to the first semi. Brick emptied it, and

Beckett went in. Sitting down in front of the box, she smiled. "Hello, Mr. Jones. I believe you know who I am."

"Miss Angelo, I'm afraid I can't defend you for the murder of Julian."

She chuckled. "Well, here's the thing, I won't be tried for his murder. I'm sure my father and Marcel have informed you of the fact that I have an eidetic memory. I'm trading what knowledge I have for my freedom, and you are going to help me by answering some questions. Why did you come to get Joey out of jail, when you knew Marcel was dead?" He just sat there looking at her. She smiled. "It's all right, I already figured it out. You told Julian that Marco was alive. I know you were going to get Joey out, so he could finish the job Julian started twenty years ago."

"Joey who?"

Beckett laughed. "Joey Malone. Mr. Jones, I know you are in possession of a letter that Marcel wrote for Marco. I'd like it please."

"It's in my briefcase. How did you know when everyone believed him to be dead?"

"I didn't." She smiled. "If I were you, I'd help these men out with what they need. You are the keeper of the secrets for this family. Don't worry. I gave them all the names of everyone, so you'll be safe." Beckett got up. "One more thing. Where is the biometric safe Marcel had installed?"

Jones looked at her. "The bathroom in his office, behind the mirror."

"Thank you." Beckett opened the door. "Mr. Brick, may I talk to you?" Brick climbed into the truck. "Mr. Jones has something in his briefcase that I want. Would you please get it for me?"

He just stood there looking at her. "I'm afraid that's evidence."

"Perhaps, but what I want isn't. It has nothing to do with this case, and if you want my knowledge, you'll give it to me." She smiled.

"What is it?"

"An envelope, sealed." She watched him open a door, pulling out the briefcase. He handed her the envelope. "Thank you." Walking back to the box, she held it up, and Mr. Jones nodded to her. As she passed

Brick on her way out, she said, "I believe Mr. Jones is going to be very cooperative. Isn't that right, Mr. Jones?"

"Yeah," he said.

Smiling, she looked at Brick. "I'd like to see Joey now." Folding the envelope, she put it in her back pocket. Climbing down, Marco took her hand, walking away from everyone."

"Beck, what are you doing?"

"We'll talk later when we are alone. I need to talk to Joey, and then we can go." She walked away from him, toward the last truck. When she sat down in front of him, he laughed. "You're a dead woman walking."

Beckett smiled at him. "They know who you are, Joey. They all do. Why are you here?"

"To gather information. Julian has people out there looking for you. They will find you, and I'm going to enjoy watching him kill you."

She laughed. "Didn't Mr. Jones tell you?"

"I didn't talk to him."

"Julian is dead. He didn't make it. No one is coming for me, Joey, just like no one is coming for you. You will pay for your crimes."

"The families won't have it."

"Well, here's the thing. The families will do as the head of the Lucian family says. Besides, I'm trading my freedom for the knowledge I have. The families will be no more."

He sat there looking at her. "There isn't a head. He's dead."

"Well, there's where you have been misinformed." She smiled. "Marco is now the head of the Lucian family."

He laughed. "Still believe that shit? Poor crazy Beckett."

She got up, opening the door, waving at Marco. As he walked up to the box, she moved over so Marco could see him. "Well, Joey, you look different, but I always knew you were a sick fuck."

Joey's eyes shot to Beckett. "You expect anyone to believe he's Marco Lucian? They'll kill you the minute you show your face. Julian killed Marco. I know because I was there when it happened."

Marco smiled. "You look exactly the same as Julian did when he realized it was me."

"What are you talking about?" Joey snapped at him.

Marco laughed. "I paid my brother a visit yesterday. I figured I should at least pay my respects."

Beckett looked at Marco; he could see the fire in her eyes as she nodded to him. He smiled, ran his knuckle down her jaw, and left. Turning her attention back to Joey, she said, "Marcel hid him away. Didn't you wonder how Mr. Jones found you? The deputy was hired by Marcel to watch over Marco. The deputy called Mr. Jones to report in, just like he did every month for the last twenty years. Jones came to get you out so you could kill your husband and then Marco. See, Mr. Jones fancies himself the one in charge because he knows all the secrets. But he knows it's over now. I am going to bring the Lucian crime family to its knees." She got up and left.

"Mr. Brick, may I speak to you alone?" Marco was watching as they walked back to the car. "In the Lucian home, in Marcel's office, there is a private bathroom. Behind the mirror is a biometric safe. Can you get the safe and bring it here? I believe all the information you need to end the Lucian Family is in that safe. I know Marcel, so if you try to open it, everything inside will be destroyed."

"How do you think you'll be able to open it?"

She smiled. "Just do it. If I can't open it, then I'll tell you everything. But the families are closing in, so you better hurry."

She went to walk away. "Where are you going?"

"To the place I should have been for the past twenty years. I'm going home, Mr. Brick. I'll see you in a few days. Charlie will know how to find me. I won't be far."

Walking up to Marco and Charlie, she smiled a small smile. "We can go now." She sat in the back alone, looking out the window. She hated that this was happening. If only she had stayed at that hotel, she would never have seen him, never knew that he was alive. Her eyes moved to look at the back of his head. She had loved him her whole life, and now she was a murderer, and she was trading all her knowledge for her freedom.

He couldn't love her like she wanted, needed him to love her. He had given his whole heart to someone else, which is totally understandable. She felt a tear slip from her eye and quickly wiped it away. She was scared to the core. Joey was right; she was a dead woman walking. Beckett knew deep down that she really was all right with that. She was thirty-four, and her bones and body ached like her eighty-year-old grandmother's. There would be no more pain for her.

They pulled up to the cabin, and Marco got out and opened her door. She just stood in the snow watching Charlie pull out. "You coming, Beck?" Marco called from the cabin.

Turning, she looked at him. She wanted him before she died, but she didn't want him here. Looking around, she knew they were unprotected, isolated here. "Not here, we are too isolated out here."

Marco shut the cabin door and walked to his truck. Opening the truck door for her, she climbed in. They didn't say a word on the drive back to the cottage. They didn't say a word as Beckett moved to the bedroom, closing the door behind her. Taking the envelope and slipping it under the pillow, she took a shower. As she walked out, wrapped in a towel, Marco was sitting on the bed.

Beckett didn't think about what she was doing when she moved toward him, climbed on his lap, and straddled him. "I don't know what is going to happen to me."

"Well, Brick let you go, so they must know you can run."

She giggled. "I gave them a great deal of information in those three conversations."

His hands rested on her hips. "Sweetheart, you do realize you have nothing on but a towel."

"Do I make you nervous?"

"Beck, no. I can't do this."

She heard the pain in his voice, and her heart hurt for him. She moved off his lap and sat on the bed next to him. "I'm sorry." She bumped his shoulder.

"It's me who needs to apologize. I shouldn't have touched you the way I have. I shouldn't take liberties with you."

"Don't. You are the only man I've ever loved."

"Beck, I'm still in love with my wife. I'm still dealing with their deaths. But I'm still a man, and you are very beautiful, very tempting. It's been a very long time for me."

She got up, grabbed her bag of clothes, and went into the bathroom to change.

Marco was in the kitchen, making them something to eat when she walked out of the bathroom. Looking at the pillow, she grabbed the envelope and put it in her pocket. They ate, not talking. When she finished, Beckett found herself wandering around his house. The house he had shared with his wife and daughter.

She couldn't help but wonder if they would have had a life like this if he had taken her with him, or even come back for her. But Julian wouldn't have let her go. He would have found them, and then for sure they'd be dead.

So much turmoil within her. So many times, she dreamt of a life with him, and now here she was. The cosmic universe interfered, and she landed in his lap. Standing by the window, she could feel him. A small smile formed on her lips. He would never love her, not like she wanted, and she wanted to consume him. For more than twenty years of her life, she loved a man who was dead. Marco Lucian died that day, and Marc Miller was born. He wasn't the boy she loved. He was a man who loved a woman, whose death nearly ended him. That's how she wanted to be loved, how she wanted him to love her.

"You aren't Marco Lucian anymore. You aren't the boy I've loved my whole life. You grew up and became Marc Miller. I know that if you had taken me with you, or even come back for me, that we would both be dead. That this whole life I lived would be different."

"Beckett," he said.

Without turning around, she continued, "It's all right, Marco. I understand. I'm not some love-struck teenager anymore. Like you, I've lived twenty years with my dreams. I suppose the dream of you is what helped me weather the storms. It calmed my soul and gave me strength. I would convince myself that you would be proud of me every time I survived him. I know what needs to be done to save you. To protect you from certain death. Too many people know you're alive. Jones, I think, expected you to take control. He has no idea who you are, just that you are." She reached in her back pocket, pulling out the envelope. With her back to him, she unfolded it, looking at it. She knew the stationary was from Marcel's desk. "Jones had this with him. He was going to give it to Alex, who in turn would have made sure that you ended up with it."

She turned to see him leaning against the door frame. As she moved toward him, she felt her heart breaking, knowing he would never love her like she needed him to. Handing Marco the envelope, she put her hand on his chest. "You will forever be my heart. I'm going to sleep. Tomorrow promises to be a very informative day. Good night, Mr. Miller." He reached out for her, but she shook her head, her eyes not leaving his.

Marco watched her as she closed the bedroom door. He wasn't sure how he felt about the things she said to him. He saw the light go off and moved his eyes to the envelope in his hand.

He sat down on the couch, opening it, and pulled out the folded pages. Unfolding them, he knew it was from his father. He began reading.

To my son, Marco,

If you have this letter, then I am no longer drawing breath. I know that the hatred you have for me is deep. I know you think I was or am a brutal man because of the way I treated you while you were with us. It was never my intention to make you feel this way. In my own sick way, I was trying to toughen you up to take my place as the head of this family. The right should go to the oldest son, but Julian is damaged beyond anything I ever did to him, and your brother, my beloved Benny, didn't have the heart, he was more like your mother, God rest her soul. She had the kindest heart of any woman I ever encountered in my life. My heart was broken when she left this earth.

I know you think or believe that I had a hand in her death, but it's just the opposite. She was my match in every way. I like the risky ways in the bedroom, and she was just like me. I know you don't want to hear the details, and I'm not going to give them to you. But I also know that you heard what you believed was me hurting her. I would never, nor had I ever hurt her. When I would slap her or shove her away from me, it was the anger deep inside of me. I never wanted to be this man. When it was all said and done, her arms were the ones that held me when I cried for hurting you, for hurting her. She was the only good thing in my life. I didn't choose this life. It was inherited, just as it would have been for you.

I know you think your mother gave her life to protect you, but it wasn't only your mother. We both decided to let you go, to let you survive. After what Julian did to you, I let him and everyone else believe that he killed you. He would have in the end.

He is the one who ended your mother's life. He knew that you were the chosen son. He cornered your mother one night while he was too drunk to remember and hurt her badly, trying to get the truth out of her. I was unfortunately away on business. When I returned, I found her at the foot of the stairs, and her injuries were extreme. I paid off the newspaper to say she was a victim of a robbery. He's my son, just like you are, and just like I protected you, I protected him. My mistake. But in this family, you do what is required of you to do.

For years, I watched him and planned his demise, a horrible thing for a father to say about his child, but he had his clan of boys who thought he walked on water, and I couldn't end six lives as well as his, so I let it play out. When he took Benny from me, sweet innocent Benny, I knew that he was coming for me next. He wanted to be King, and he wanted no one in his way. With you gone, your mother gone, and Benny gone, nothing was in his way except for me.

Julian was so far into drugs and the sex trade; he was in deep and wanted the family to join in his profitable endeavors. Those are things I would never do, and he knew it. So, he set out on his mission to end my life.

When we sent you away that night, I had already hired Alex to be your shadow. He was young in this world, and no one knew him, so he was the perfect choice. I know you sat outside of Angelo's house until just before sunrise. I know you wanted to take little Beckett with you, but I am grateful that you didn't. She was promised to Julian, but I couldn't let that happen. I forbid him from taking her before she was his wife, and then I forbid him to marry her until I was done running the family. I did my best to save the girl you loved. I hope I succeeded, and she is still whole.

Marco, there are a few things I need you to know. I was at your wedding when you married Katherine. I saw what you saw in her. She was so much like Beckett that it was as if you were with her doppelganger. I couldn't have been happier for you. She was a good choice. She would have taken this world by storm.

But when the accident happened and you lost everything, I was there with you. I sat by your bed for days while you lay in a coma. I held your hand, and I prayed to your mother to let you live. I buried your beautiful wife, daughter, and son. I don't think I ever felt like that before. I know how I felt when your mother left me, so I knew how you were going to feel. I wanted to make it better for you. You made a life for yourself, and you have grown into a very powerful man.

I have missed you every day, but I knew you were fine and doing a wonderful job, growing into the man you are today. That Charlie Jamison is a hell of a man. No, I never approached him, never had a conversation with him. I never interfered with anything to do with the life you made for yourself. I wish that I could have been the man who shaped you, but I couldn't have made a better choice of a man to bring you into manhood.

My health is failing. I've been to the doctor, and it seems I am slowly being poisoned. I know it's Julian, and I am not going to do anything to stop this. I never wanted to be the head of this family, and I know I will never have a relationship with you. Your mother and Benny are gone, and to be honest, I wanted to be with her since the moment she left. So, I am going to let him kill me, let him slowly poison me. I deserve the pain, and I deserve the punishment.

But I have taken precautions. Remember when you were twelve and Julian broke your arm? Well, while we were at the hospital, I had the doctor *draw your blood. In my bathroom, in my office, which will be yours if you want to claim your head at the table, is evidence against Julian and his crew, that will put him away for the rest of his life. There is also everything you will need to end the Lucian Family. It's my gift of freedom to you. The ultimate gift. The safe is biometric, so you will need your blood, your fingerprint, and your eye scan to open it. Only Jones knows it's there.*

Find Beckett and save her from Julian. Give her the life you wanted her to have while you sat outside her house and dreamed in your head. Katherine would want you to move on. I know she would because she is just like Beckett.

You are my son, my youngest son, and you are the one I am most proud of. Sending you away was the only right thing I have done in this life, outside of marrying your mother. I have always loved you, Marco, even when you believed I didn't. Even when you hated me the most, I loved you. I will always love you.

Now, make the right choice for you. Make the best choice for Beckett. That woman has lived through a hell I wouldn't wish on a dead dog. She is strong, and she will love you for the rest of your life. Hell, she has loved you her whole life.

I love you, Marco.

Your father,

Marcel Lucian

He didn't realize he was crying until a tear fell on the paper, smearing the ink. Marco laid the letter on the table, then leaned back against the couch and closed his eyes. Flashes of memory filled his mind. He remembered feeling a hand holding his as he began to wake up after the accident. It felt familiar to him, but not. He thought about their wedding; he was so happy, and Katherine was so beautiful that nothing else mattered to him.

Marco did have the life he wanted. As he sat there thinking about the hate he'd felt throughout his whole life for his father, he realized that he only hated him because he had never felt love from him. Marcel was a cold-hearted, hardcore, son of a bitch.

He looked at the letter again; those words told a different story, but none of it really mattered anymore. He would never become the head of the family. It wasn't in Marco to be cruel or violent.

Standing in the doorway, he looked at Beckett, lying in his bed, and let his mind wander to Katherine. As the memories of their life together flashed through his mind, he couldn't find the comparisons to Beckett. He didn't really know the woman before him anymore because she'd lived twenty years without him. She'd been just a child when he left, just like him.

Maybe his father was right about them, about Katherine and Beckett being so similar. Marco knew that Beckett held a piece of his heart, a piece he never gave away. Katherine was right; she never had it all. Shaking his head, he knew she had it. Katherine had all of him. But if that was true, then why did he feel this woman to the core of his being? She was so broken, so destroyed by the life she'd been dealt. Could he do this with her? Could he continue through life with her? Could he love her completely, like he loved Katherine?

While pulling the door shut, he saw Beckett move, so he paused. "Marco?"

"Yes, go back to sleep, sweetheart."

"I wasn't sleeping. You all right?"

He chuckled. "I haven't been all right for a long time. You get some sleep." He pulled the door closed and went back to the couch.

Beckett got up, pulled a t-shirt over her head, and followed him into the living room. She saw the letter on the table and looked at Marco. "Was it bad?"

Turning, he looked at her. "It was both of my parents that helped me leave. He knew everything. He knew how I felt about you. He was at my wedding. He was even at the hospital after the accident. He buried Katherine and my kids. Why didn't you tell me that Julian killed my mother?"

She closed her eyes and dipped her head before explaining, "I'm sorry. There's just so much, and I think I'm still in shock that I'm here with you."

"Julian wanted you so badly that he killed our father to have you."

"I know, he was going to rape me that day. I couldn't let that happen. He never broke my spirit, never took my dreams, but he would have destroyed me if he'd achieved what he wanted."

Marco put his hand out, and when Beckett slipped hers in his, he pulled her down onto the couch with him. She snuggled into his side.

"I'm not sure what to say anymore. What to do," he whispered into her hair. "I don't know how to do this, Beck. I loved her so much, but part of my heart has always belonged to you. I never gave it to her. Now, here you are, in my arms, and that part of my heart that has stayed dark with the loss of you has woken and is burning brighter and brighter, taking over the part that loves Katherine. I'm struggling, fighting with myself, trying not to allow you to take the love I have for her away."

Beckett snuggled closer to him. "I don't ever want, nor would I expect you to forget them or stop loving them. I never forgot you. I never stopped loving you. It takes time to move forward, to learn to breathe again. Marco, I don't expect anything from you. When this is over, I'll go into witness protection, and we will never see each other again. It's enough for me just knowing you are alive."

"Aww, Beck." He rolled to his side, wrapping his leg around her hip. "I'm not so sure I could let you go."

Beckett kissed his throat and said, "You will. It'll be the same as it was twenty years ago, only this time we'll each know that the other is alive and safe."

"But will we be happy?"

"Happy to be alive. Happy to be free."

"Sleep, sweetheart. I got you," he whispered.

Her arm wrapped around his waist as she snuggled closer.

Marco opened his eyes. The warmth that surrounded him was something he hadn't felt in a very long time. Beckett hadn't moved all night long. Her head was still tucked under his chin, and her leg gently pressed against his balls. He was instantly hard. Half was natural, but the tightness was because of the woman in his arms. She felt right.

She moved her arm up his back as she began to wake up. "Mmm…" she moaned. Pulling back, she twisted the upper half of her body away from his, opening her eyes as he moved the hair off her face. "Good morning."

"I think it's afternoon." His eyes roved down her body, stopping on the peaked nipple poking through her t-shirt.

Her eyes stayed on him as he licked his lips. She moved her leg, pressing slightly on his balls, and he closed his eyes as a low moan vibrated in his chest. "Beck." Her name tumbled past his lips.

Marco struggled not to touch her. He wanted, no, needed to touch her. Spreading his fingers, he let just the tips touch her breast. It was when she covered his hand with hers that his moan turned into a growl, and she slid his hand to cover her breast completely. He didn't do the right thing and stop. He couldn't; she felt so damn good. They lay there kissing, her leg applying the perfect amount of pressure to his balls. He caressed her, pinching her nipple.

Marco pulled back, his hand still gently caressing her. "Beck."

"No, don't stop, Marco. Please." Her voice sounded strangled as his hand squeezed her.

"Beck, I can't, not yet. I'm not ready."

She pressed into his balls with her thigh. Marco's eyes rolled in his head. Then he felt her hand on him. "Marco," she moaned as his mouth covered hers. She pressed his erection against his body as she moved her hand slowly along his shaft.

Marco let go of her breast and slowly pulled her hand away. "No, sweetheart. It wouldn't mean anything right now except a release. It's not what I'm willing to do. Katherine is still in me. It would be her face I would see; it would be her body. I don't want to do that to you. Do you understand?"

She nodded. "Will we ever get there?"

"I don't know." His thumb ran across her bottom lip. "I don't know. We need to get up. I need to call my partner. I was supposed to go back to work today." He moved to get up, adjusting his cock. Picking up his phone, he called Kyle. "Hey, listen, I'm going to take a few more days. A childhood friend is in town for another week."

"Not a problem, we've got this covered. Take all the time you need. You sure you're all right?"

"I'm getting there. Thanks, buddy."

"Maybe we could get dinner or something, or grab a beer."

Marco laughed. "I think I drank enough for the rest of my life. Haven't had one in eight days."

"Well, a cup of coffee then."

"Thanks, Kyle. We'll talk soon."

After disconnecting the phone, he scrolled through to Charlie's number as he made coffee.

"Hey, what's up?"

"Visitors, and not the good kind."

Marco froze and didn't say anything. He disconnected the call and went looking for Beckett. "Come on," he said in a hushed whisper. Taking her hand, they moved quietly through the house, grabbing her coat and boots. Marco moved his desk. "Do you trust me?" She nodded. He opened the hatch in the floor, then picked her up and set her in the compartment. "Get down and don't make a sound," he whispered.

The fear he saw in her eyes gutted him. Tears silently fell from her eyes as she knelt down in the hole and then laid down. Marco struggled, watching her shake, to put the cover back on, and then moved his desk back.

He went to get his coffee and was leaning against the counter when he saw two men walk past the window. "What the fuck?" Grabbing a knife, he slipped it in his back pocket and pulled his shirt down over it before opening the back door. "Excuse me, can I help you with something?"

"Are you Marc Miller?"

"Who's asking?"

The guy pulled out a badge. "Lance Michaels, F.B.I."

Marco nearly laughed. "What can I do for you?"

"We're looking for this woman."

The guy handed Marco a picture of Beckett. "Miss Evans? Why?"

"She's wanted for murder. Is she here?"

"No. I picked her up at the hospital and gave her some money, then took her to the bus station over in Boise."

"May we come in and look around?"

"Do you have a warrant?"

The two men looked at each other. "No, we don't."

"Well, when you get one, come back. Then you can come in and look around. Have a nice day." Marco shut the door and locked it. He waited for them to leave before he moved to the front of the house. They got in a black car and just sat there. He called Charlie. "Who are they?"

"Don't know, but I can guess."

"They're sitting in front of my house. I can't get her out of here."

"Sit tight, the boys are back in town. We're on our way."

Marco moved his desk, opening the floor. Beckett was curled up like a baby. His heart swelled when he saw her look up at him. She grabbed his hand when he reached in, and Marco pulled her out and into his arms. "I'm sorry." Beckett clung to him while she silently cried. His hold didn't waver. He moved away, closing the floor and moving his desk back into place. Then he wrapped himself around her, moving to the side of the window to watch.

Charlie, along with four other cars pulled up and surrounded the black car. "Go into the bedroom. I'll be right back."

Beckett nodded, and Marco headed outside. Charlie met him at the bottom of the driveway. "They aren't F.B.I.?" Marco asked.

"Nope, members of the family. They're looking for her."

"Thanks for the heads up."

Charlie chuckled. "You would have had more time if you'd answered the phone."

He smiled. "I was sleeping." He stepped off the curb, moving toward Mr. Brick. "Friends of yours?" he smarted.

"Nope. Maybe yours?"

"Same transport as before? They had time to call it in. More will be here," Marco said.

"We've got a few guys that can be trusted."

"Do you mind?" Marco nodded to the two men.

"Be my guest."

Walking up, he said, "I guess since you're not F.B.I., I can only assume you are here on behalf of someone else. I know it's not Julian," he watched their eyes, "because he's dead. So, who sent you all the way up here?" Neither man said a word to him. "It's all good. These gentlemen are going to make sure you make it all the way home to stand trial."

Marco turned to walk away, when one of the men said, "You can't hide her forever. She murdered Julian Lucian. Who are you?"

Marco laughed. "Better Julian than Miss Evans. She is far better looking." He walked away.

Brick smiled. "Not going to tell them who you really are?"

"I'm just Marc Miller, nobody special."

Charlie laughed. "We have some business. The lake?"

"Here is good. Give me a few." Marco nodded as he continued into the cottage. He shut and locked the door. When he walked into the bedroom, Beckett was curled up on the bed silently crying. As he pulled her into his arms, she uncurled herself, and Marco wrapped himself around her. "They're gone, sweetheart."

"They'll be back." She sniffled.

"It'll be over soon, and you will be free."

"The family is huge. The ties are deep and strong. I'll never be free."

"Aww, Beck, we'll be fine. I am, after all, the head of the family now. If they won't stop, I'll make them stop."

"No, Marco. No one needs to know about you."

"And no one needs to know about you," he whispered. "As comfortable as I am, we need to go. Charlie needs to talk to us."

"To you," she said into his neck.

"To us. We are in this together now. Until the end."

"What if the end is death?"

"Then it's death. Either way, it'll be over." He kissed her forehead, and they got up.

Marco went to open the door, and then Brick, Jay, and Charlie walked in. Two other men carried in a box and set on the floor. When they took off their shoes, the box was moved to the coffee table. "What's this?" Marco said.

"Hopefully, it's the end," Beckett said from the bedroom door. Everyone turned to look at her. "I take it my information was correct?"

"It was. It wasn't easy getting it out," Brick answered.

Marco watched as the two men took the safe out of the box. He looked at Beckett. "How did you know?"

"My father," she said softly, moving into the room. "It's biometric. Your blood, your fingerprint, and a retinal scan will open it. If I'm wrong, then this is going to take a very long time."

"Shall we give it a try?" Brick asked.

Beckett moved to the table; Marco stood watching her examine the safe. She looked up at him. "If I'm right, what's in here should be more than enough to end this. Enough to keep you safe, to make you free."

His eyes locked on hers. "What about you?" His words were soft. No one moved. He was sure no one was breathing; he knew he wasn't.

She shrugged her shoulders, and her voice sounded small. "I don't matter. I killed him."

Marco shook his head. "You were defending yourself."

"It's my word against the facts. I think it was all supposed to happen this way. Marco, my life means nothing. My parents are gone, and I have nothing. He took everything from me."

Shaking his head, he moved toward her. "He didn't take you."

"No, but he took you away from me. You have a life here. Please, just open the safe."

"Not if it means you leave. Beck..." He reached for her.

"No. Please, Marco, I can't." Her words came out as a whisper. "Just open it."

He smiled as he pushed his hand into her hair, wrapping his fingers around her head. "Not until you promise not to leave."

"It's not up to me. They won't stop coming for me. If they figure out who you are, they will hunt you, and I can't let that happen." Tears fell onto her cheeks. "You were supposed to be dead."

Marco saw movement, and it pulled him from her. He looked at Brick. "She gets full immunity, and we get around the clock protection until it's over."

Brick smiled. "Mr. Miller, she murdered Julian Lucian."

"In self-defense. That is my deal, or this is not going to happen."

"Marco," Beckett touched his chest, "don't. It's fine. Whatever they say or do, it's fine. I have nothing. I am nothing."

He took her hand and pulled her into the bedroom. Leaning against the door, he watched her. "Beck," his voice was strangled with fear and pain, "you are someone to me."

She shook her head. "I was at one time. Now, I'm just your past."

"No!" he shouted. "No, Beck. You are my now, my future."

She stepped forward, putting her hand on his chest. "We don't have a future, Marco. You'll never love me like I want or need you to love me. Your life will go on, just as it has for the last twenty years. You'll forget me again."

He felt the tears form in his eyes. "No, Beck, I never forgot you."

She smiled. "Marco, it's fine. It was different for me. I didn't know you were alive. I understand why you didn't come back for me. We need to do this. No matter what the end results are. We need to end it." She reached behind him, turning the door handle. Marco moved as she pulled the door open. "Come on," she said softly, taking his hand.

When they walked into the living room, Marco's eyes met Brick's. "We have a deal, Mr. Miller. If the contents of the safe and Miss Angelo's knowledge are enough to end the family, we have a deal."

"And if it's not?" Marco asked.

"How about we cross that bridge when we come to it? Why don't we open this safe? Let's take this one step at a time. I think we need to start putting the pieces of this puzzle together. Build a game plan."

"Go on," Beckett said as she let go of his hand. "Blood, fingerprint, ocular scan. In that order."

Marco sat down in front of the safe. Pulling his knife from his pocket, he poked his finger and placed it over the little hole until a drop of blood dripped in. The first green light clicked on. Next, he put his thumb on the pad, and it scanned his print. The second green light went on. "Which eye?" he asked.

"The right one," Beckett said.

"But my father was left-handed. Wouldn't it be the left eye?" Beckett nodded, and Marco leaned forward, placing his left eye in front of the scanner. The third light turned on. It was so quiet in the room as everyone listened to the tumblers turning, and then there was a swishing sound as the safe unlocked.

Marco reached for the door, his hand shaking as he pulled the door open. He could see books, ledgers of some kind. Taking them out one by one, he sat them on the table. No one in the room moved. There were several boxes, so he pulled them out and opened each one, finding pieces of his mother's jewelry. The last box held her wedding rings.

Marco picked up two envelopes. Inside the first one was pictures of his life over the past twenty years—his wife, daughter, the sign for their construction company. He could feel his heart slamming in his chest when he came upon the ultrasound of baby Joseph and one of Angela. His tears fell silently as he carefully put them back in the envelope. "These are mine," he said, taking the envelopes. He got up and went to the bedroom. Beckett watched him, wanting to go with him, but she knew he was with the ghosts of his past.

Marco slid down the door, his hand covering his mouth as he cried. His father knew everything about him. He had hated him his whole life. Marco believed him to be a monster. He couldn't understand why he let him go, why he helped him leave. His heart hurt for them. He wanted them back. He wanted Katherine. She was so strong; she would know what to do. His head fell against the door, his eyes closed, and he felt her as his body filled with warmth. He could imagine her voice in his mind telling him to let them go. "I love you," he whispered.

Wiping his face, he opened the second envelope. Inside was a bank statement with his name on it, from a bank in the Cayman Islands. His eyes were blurry from his tears, so he wiped them, not believing what he first saw. The amount read ten million dollars. "What the fuck." Trying to put the paper back in the envelope, he met some resistance. Marco looked inside, finding yet another envelope. When he opened it, his heart nearly stopped.

My Dearest Marco,

I'm sorry that I abandoned you, sent you away, but I knew Julian would eventually kill you. He is sick in his head. I'm not sure if it was anything your father's brutality did to him, but I believe that he was born that way.

You are my baby, my youngest, my most precious boy, and yes, you were conceived in love, just as your brothers were. I know you maybe believe that your father is a horrible man, and that I am a weak woman, but that's not the case. I love him with all that I am. He is a wonderful, kind, loving man. He never did me wrong. The pressure of being who he is was more than he could bear, and he needed to vent the anger and frustration. Not that he ever really hurt me out of anger, but it was more in the bedroom. I know these aren't words you want to associate with your parents, but we were the same behind that bedroom door. I have never once regretted any of it.

I feel as if I failed as a mother. My children were exposed to a world that they never should have been. No child should. When I married your father, we had no idea what was going to happen to him, that he was to become the head of this fucked up family. He was the third child, and the position always goes to the firstborn, but your two uncles met their demise by the hand of your grandfather. He had always wanted Marcel, just as your father wanted you. But life hasn't happened that way.

When you walked into the kitchen that night, I knew in my heart that we needed to get you out. Even your father knows Julian is insane and that we should have never protected him, ignored the things he did. He should have been institutionalized as a child.

Most of my regret in sending you away is not sending little Beckett Angelo with you. Your father and I know you loved her, probably even before you realized it. But she has been promised to Julian. It was a deal made by the devil, to seal the Angelo family with the Lucian family. There is no excuse. There are no excuses for what we did, but I needed for you to survive. You were never meant to be the head of this family. It's not in your heart to be this cold, unfeeling man that it would require to take control. I just hope in the end, you don't hate me or your father for sending you away.

If the day ever comes, find Beckett and rescue her. The money is yours. It's your inheritance, and no, my darling son, it's not dirty money. It's the money my parents left me when they passed away. Marcel and I agreed to put it away, out of the reach of the family. When we sent you away, we put your name on the account. It's the only thing I have to give you that is clean of this life. Please, take it and enjoy the life you have.

You, Marco, are my greatest accomplishment. You. Not Julian or Benny, but you. My heart was ripped from my chest when I shut the door on you and sent you away. I'm not sure I will ever recover from that moment.

Your father and I cried for the loss of you for a long time. Neither of us will be the same. A mother's love never leaves. Know that no matter what life has in store for you that I will be there with you. We both will.

I love you, my beautiful boy. I hope your life is so much more than what it was. I hope that one day you and Beckett find your way back to one another. She is your match, Marco. I knew it for many years. The two of you were inseparable as you grew up. Sending you away nearly killed her. I suppose I'm thankful for the one thing Julian did do, and that was to keep her under his watchful eyes because I'm sure she would have joined you in death.

I love you, son, from the moment you were conceived, you have been our greatest accomplishment.

Have a beautiful life, my love. You are my heart.

Always,

Mom

Marco sat reading the words over and over. Everything he felt or thought about his parents was wrong. His heart hurt. With tears, he folded the pages and put them back in the envelope along with the bank statement. He slipped them under the mattress, then washed his face. When he walked out into the living room, all eyes turned to him. He put on his boots, grabbed his coat, looked at Beckett, and walked out the door.

As he drove, he couldn't breathe. He was so confused. Stopping his truck alongside the road, he got out. He had unknowingly driven to the place where his life ended. He fixed the three crosses as he cried from the pain searing his heart. When he finished, he sat down in the snow.

It was the arm around him that triggered the flood gates. Charlie had followed him. As the older man pulled him into his embrace, Marco let it go, sobbing like a child. Charlie held him while they sat in the snow, on the cliff where his dreams were broken. Where his life was interrupted.

CHAPTER NINE

Charlie saw his face when he walked out the door. There was no mistaking the pain that was clearly visible. "Please, excuse me," he said as he stood, then looked at Jay. "Don't leave her alone. They will be back for her. She's not safe." Jay nodded as Charlie pulled on his boots. His eyes connected with Beckett's. He saw the fear and pain in hers. He wasn't sure what was going on, but he knew that whatever was in those envelopes broke Marco.

Charlie headed to the cabin, but he found Marco sitting in the snow where the accident happened. When he got to him, he was in a full meltdown. Charlie wrapped his arm around the man who he helped raise. Marco let it go when he embraced him. Charlie didn't say anything; there weren't words to console Marco's grief. No man should ever have to survive something like this.

As he calmed down, he pulled away from Charlie. Blowing his nose, he chuckled. "Sorry about that."

"Marco, I can't assume I know what you are going through. There is no need to apologize. On top of all the loss you've endured, your past has now found you. It must be so overwhelming for you."

Marco shook his head. "I had it all wrong. All of it. My parents saved me because they loved me. I've spent my life hating my father for the things he did. The things I believed he'd done to my mother." He felt the tears building again. "He was at our wedding. He was here when Angela was born. He was here when we had our accident. He said he sat by my bed while I was in a coma, holding my hand. I remember someone, but then again, I don't. He buried my wife and children. He knew about you, Charlie. He praised you, giving you credit for making me the man I am. That wasn't the man I knew. The man I knew, the man I thought I was running from was a bastard. He forbade Julian from touching Beckett, from marrying her, for me. He knew we loved each other, but I forgot all about her," he cried.

"I don't think you forgot her; I think Katherine filled the emptiness you had in you. Marco, you always put on a brave face, but anyone who knew you could see that it was all just a mask. It wasn't until you met Katherine that you came to life. She just took over and made you come alive. I see it again now with Beckett, only it's different this time."

"Charlie, I love my wife and kids."

He put his arm around Marco's shoulder. "No one is saying that you don't. But they are gone, son. Beckett has always been the one. I knew that the day I gave you her license." He chuckled. "Your whole body changed when you saw her name. When you looked at me, I saw a light in your eyes I have never seen before. It's all right, Marco, to let them go. It's all right to be happy again. Katherine would want this for you, just as you would want it for her and the kids if it was you who died that day."

"I don't know if I can let them go."

"You've already started. I noticed you finally took off your ring. The changes to the cottage. Marco, you are already letting go. It's perfectly natural."

Marco sat there looking at the wheels of the buried car at the bottom of the ravine. "Thanks, Charlie."

"I'm always here for you. Marco, you don't always need to carry the weight of the world on your shoulders. It's all right to let others help you."

"Like Beckett?"

Charlie chuckled "Personally, I think you'll have your hands full with her. That girl has spunk."

Marco laughed. "Yeah, she does."

"Listen, I'm going to head back. These old bones weren't meant to sit in the snow. I'll keep my eye on her until you're ready to come back."

"Thanks, Charlie."

"I'm always here." Charlie got up. "Marco, don't stay out here too long. It's just too damn cold."

Marco nodded. "I won't."

Long after Charlie left, Marco sat in the snow. His mind was clouded with his thoughts. He loved Katherine to the point of madness, but Beckett was bringing light into his darkness. She had been his life preserver for so long. She was all he'd wanted; his plans always included her. His father was right. Katherine was a lot like Beckett, so much so that he replaced Beckett with Katherine. And she was right that he had forgotten her. His heart didn't, but his mind had.

Standing, he dusted the snow off looked at the three crosses, and smiled. "I will always love you. Thank you, Kate, for loving me. It's time. You will always be in my heart."

He got in his truck and headed back to the cottage, back to the rest of his life.

When Charlie walked into Marco's house, all eyes turned to him. His eyes focused on Beckett. "Listen, when Marco gets back, why don't we move this to my house? I think Marco and Beckett have some things to talk about. Mr. Brick, do you have a few trusted men to hang out here? They will be back, and there really isn't any place for them to hide."

Jay looked at Charlie. "What about the cabin?"

"Too isolated."

Brick agreed. "After we read through all of this, we're going to need to discuss it all with you, Miss Angelo."

Beckett nodded.

On the drive back, Marco knew his future was now with Beckett. He had loved her his whole life, but when Katherine came into his world, he forgot and let her love consume him. Pulling onto his street, he noticed two extra cars that weren't there when he left. He called Charlie as he drove past his house.

"Everything all right?" Charlie asked.

"We have company. Give her the ledgers. Under my mattress are two envelopes. Get them and take her out the back. Meet me where you dropped us off. Do it now!"

Charlie hung up and reached for the ledgers. He said to Beckett, "Coat, boots, now." Then to Brick, he said, "They're here. She is leaving, and these are going with her."

They all stood, moving to the windows while Charlie grabbed the envelopes. He and Beckett ran out the back door, meeting Marco two blocks over.

Charlie got in the truck with them. "Go to my house. Park a block over."

"I need to get her out of here."

"Marco, trust me. Just go to my house."

Beckett sat slumped down in the backseat shaking. She knew her time on this planet was limited. When Marco stopped the truck, he turned to look at her. "You go with Charlie. This isn't about freeing me, Beck. It's about saving you. I know I wouldn't survive losing you."

The tears came. "But what about you?"

He smiled, reaching to wipe her tears. "I'm just me. Now go."

He watched Charlie and Beckett get out and run. He waited until they were out of sight, and then he headed back to his house. Pulling into the driveway, he was very aware of eyes watching him.

"What just happened?" Brick asked.

"We have a bit of company," Marco explained. He watched as they all walked out of the house. Marco opened the floor and dropped the ledgers and his envelopes into the compartment. Looking at the safe, he closed the floor, then shut the safe, listening to it lock. The three red lights came on, and he wiped his thumbprint off the pad. When he walked outside, Brick had eight men standing beside the cars. "Friends of yours?" he asked Brick.

Brick laughed. "Nope."

"Do you mind?" Marco nodded at them.

"Be my guest."

Marco walked over to the men with a smile on his face. He was going to have some fun. "Let me guess, you fools are here looking for Miss Evans?" None of them said a word. "You think she killed Julian Lucian, your boss?" One of them looked at him, so Marco walked up to him. Leaning in, he said, "She did the family a favor. She did me a favor." Pulling back, he looked the guy in the eyes. "Do you know who I am?"

"You're a dead man," the guy growled out, which got the attention of the other men, who all looked at Marco. Marco swung, shocking everyone when he knocked the guy out. He chuckled, knowing he didn't use half of his strength. Looking at the rest of the men, he told them, "You should get your facts straight. Miss Evans is under my protection now."

"We won't stop coming," one guy shouted.

Marco turned, moving to him. "Then you have a problem, because either you will all end up like this or dead. It doesn't matter to me. This family is done." Leaning in, he whispered so only he could hear him, "My father was the last Don, the last boss of this family." When he pulled back, he saw the guy actually looked scared. "Now, I would suggest you cooperate with these fine gentlemen, just like Mr. Jones and Mr. Malone did."

The guy laughed. "Fuck you, asshole."

Marco swung, knocking him out, then looked at the six remaining men. "Julian would want you to do this, to atone for his crimes, his sins. He wanted me to tell you to be good little soldiers and accept the inevitable, that this party is over." Turning, Marco headed back to Brick and Jay, who were smiling.

"Who the hell are you?" one of the men called out.

Marco winked at Jay, then turned and said, "I'm the new boss." He moved past Brick. "That should make them wonder. Would you secure them so Beckett can talk to them if she wants?"

"You got it," Brick said.

Jay, Brick, and the other two men came into the cottage when the excitement was over. Marco was in the kitchen making coffee. He was shocked at how easy it was for him to hurt those men. Flashbacks of the brutality he suffered from his father and his brother were raging in his mind.

He knew deep inside that he would give everything he had to save her. While sitting out there on the road earlier, he had accepted the fact that Beckett still had his heart. Both of his parents knew it. Marco was confused by these new facts he had learned about them. He was beginning to understand why his father did what he did. He knew this was going to be a fight to the death, and for the first time in a year, he hoped it wasn't his or Beckett's.

Brick interrupted his thoughts. "I've got a few more men coming."

Marco turned to look at him. "I've been thinking. The people of this town don't deserve this shit storm that is obviously coming. Charlie is like a father to me. We need to get out of here. Make the arrangements. I'll get Beckett and the journals and meet you at the airport."

"I have a place where you'll be safe in Chicago."

"That's fine, but I'm going to need a truck and a few guns. This is going to get ugly. Better to end it where it all started. I'll see you in an hour." Brick nodded and they left.

Marco locked the door behind them. He packed some clothes in a bag, along with the clothes he'd bought for Beckett. As he was closing the closet, he saw the picture of Katherine. Picking it up, he touched her face. "I will always love you, beautiful." Bringing the picture to his lips, he kissed it before gently putting it back and closing the door. He knew now that he could let them go. He loved Beckett; he had always loved her. It was time to end this, to save her, to save him.

He grabbed everything out of the hole, then pulled out his phone and called Kyle. "Hey, I'm leaving town for a while. Not sure when I'll be back."

"Marco, what's going on? I had some guys come to the job site asking questions about you and some girl. Is everything all right?"

Marco laughed. "Don't worry about it. I'll tell you everything when I get back. Thanks, buddy."

"No problem. You take care of yourself."

"You too."

Macro called Charlie. "Charlie, listen, would you take Beckett to the airport? Brick and Jay are waiting there for her. I'll meet you there. I need to end this, and I won't do it here. These guys are going to keep coming, and I won't bring a war here."

"Are you sure about this?"

Marco sighed. "Nope. But it needs to end. Just make sure she gets on that plane. Call me when it's done. I'm pretty sure I'll be followed there, so hopefully, when they see me leave, they'll follow and leave town."

"Marco, come home when this is over. Don't do anything stupid."

"Charlie, I think I found a reason to live again."

"Good for you. We'll leave right now."

Marco waited for fifteen minutes and then left after putting his bags in the truck. As he drove through town, he noticed a car following him. He couldn't wipe the smile off his face.

When he got out of the truck at the airport, he watched the car drive by. Shaking his head as his phone buzzed, he knew Beckett was on the plane. After grabbing the bags, he headed toward her.

Beckett was sitting in the back row by the window. When their eyes connected, he felt her fear. His heart jumped when she gave him a small smile. He couldn't get to her fast enough. Reaching for her, he wrapped his arm around her, pulling her into his embrace as he sat down. She was shaking. "I got you now. We are going to end this once and for all."

Beckett didn't say anything. Brick was watching them. Marco looked at him, and Brick smiled and nodded, closing his eyes. Marco buried his head in Beckett's neck. He was scared shitless. He needed to free her.

～

After Beckett calmed down, she pulled her head back, touching her fingers to his face. "Why would you do this?"

"I'm not ready to lose you again. I don't think I'll ever be ready," he whispered.

"But..." Marco pulled her to him, kissing her.

"No buts, Beck. No buts. We are in this 'til the end. Now, I need to talk to Jay and Brick. You can stay here or come with me."

She smiled, looking around. "It's not a big plane. I'll stay." She sat there looking into his eyes. For the first time since they'd been reunited, she saw a sense of peace in them. Somehow, she knew they were going to be all right. As she moved to her own seat, Marco's hands didn't leave her body, nor did his eyes. She smiled at him. "Go on, I'm fine."

He smiled. "You're shaking."

Whispering, she said, "I'm scared. Marco, is going back the smartest choice?"

"Those people are my friends. They don't deserve the war the family is bringing. The only way to fight is on their home ground." He kissed her temple. "I'll be back. Try and get some rest."

Nodding, she watched him move toward Brick. Marco picked up a bag and set it on the table. "Some evidence for you."

Beckett nearly shit when he pulled out a brick of drugs. "Julian's?" Brick asked.

"Yep." Reaching into another bag, he pulled out the journals. "Keep these. Figure this shit out." He turned to go back to Beckett. "Oh, and I want to go to Julian's funeral. The families should be there out of respect."

Brick chuckled, shaking his head.

Marco was watching Beckett; her body cringed when he said he was going to Julian's funeral. When he sat down, she looked out the window. "I'm not going with you."

"Oh, I know you're not."

"Why would you do this? Why are we putting ourselves in the middle of this?"

"Something my father said. Beck, if we run, they won't stop. They don't know who I am."

"Yet." She turned to look at him when she spoke, her voice nearly inaudible, "They will kill you. I can't live through that again."

Tilting her head to look into her eyes, he told her, "Beck, they won't kill me. I won't let them. Come here." He reached around her, pulling her onto his lap. "How about we go on a trip when this is done? Get to know each other again?"

She giggled as she snuggled into his embrace. "I'd like that."

When they landed, Marco and Beckett were ushered into a black SUV with nearly blacked-out windows and taken to an apartment in downtown Chicago. Once inside, Brick said, "I live in the adjoining apartment. This door," he walked over to a door by the front door, "goes into my place. You'll be safe here. Get some rest. Julian's funeral is tomorrow at nine. I'll make sure you have a suit to wear."

"Black suit, black shirt, black tie, black shoes." He walked over, opened the backpack, pulled out ten grand, and handed the cash to Brick. "Spare no expense." He gave Brick his sizes. "Oh, and I'll need four black roses and six men that the family doesn't know." Brick laughed. "You want me to play the part, let's play. This needs to end. The sooner the better."

Brick left. Marco and Beckett stood looking at each other. "Please don't do this."

"Beck," he whispered. "Why don't you get some rest."

She stepped into him, wrapping her arms around his waist. "Come and rest with me."

Marco wrapped his arms around her. "Aww, Beck." They stood holding each other. Taking his hand, Beckett started walking to the bedroom. Marco stopped. "I can't, but how about we lay on the couch?" Beckett stood there looking at him, finally smiling, but he could see the confusion in her eyes. "Come on." He led her to the couch, tucking her between him and the back. Marco made sure he was wrapped around her. He knew she was scared because he was freaking out.

Marco knew what needed to be done. He knew the only way any of this was going to work was if his presence forced a ripple effect through the family. He needed them to question everything. He needed for them to make mistakes so Brick could end this mess and save her. Closing his eyes, he let the warmth of Beckett fill him. He knew he needed her as much, if not more than she needed him.

Morning came faster than Marco wanted. He hadn't slept like that in a very long time, but the knock on the door woke him up. He didn't want to move, but he knew what was on the agenda for the day—his brother's funeral and making himself known to the family. A big day indeed.

Unfolding himself from Beckett, he stood and looked at her. His heart warmed, filling the darkness with light. The knock came again.

Opening the door, he found Brick holding his suit in one hand and a few bags in the other. "It's seven now, and we'll be ready in an hour." Handing Marco the bags, he smiled. "You sure about this?"

Marco laughed. "You're the one who thought this was a good idea. Did you get the black roses?" Brick nodded. "The car needs to be untraceable, no government plates if this is going to work."

"In the bag is a Kevlar vest. Make sure you put it on. There is a double shoulder holster in there as well. I'll give you the guns when we get in the car."

After his shower, he stood in the bedroom in his boxer briefs looking at the suit on the bed when movement caught his attention. Turning his head, he saw Beckett leaning against the wall, looking at him with her bottom lip tucked between her teeth. His smile was automatic. "Sweetheart, what are you doing?"

"Marco," her voice sounded breathy, "you are most definitely not the boy I once knew."

He laughed, moving to stand in front of her, then tilted her head to look into her eyes. "No, I'm not." When she licked her lips, his hand slid into her hair and his mouth covered hers. Beckett moved her hands from his stomach up his chest to wrap around his shoulders. He moaned from deep within as his hands caressed her body and his thumbs brushed her nipples. As his hands raked over her ass, he cupped it firmly, then he bent to pick her up and pressed her against the wall.

Their kiss was deep, hard, but passionate. Marco was fully hard when Beckett pulled away. "Definitely not the boy," she moaned.

Marco laughed. "Did you sleep well?"

She nodded, her eyes moving to the bed. "Do you have to do this?"

"I do. I want you free."

Her fingers trailed along his lips. "What about you?"

He kissed her fingers as he set her down. He watched her eyes move down his body to his erection. "As long as you are free," he tilted her head up, "I'll be free." He moved away from her and proceeded to get dressed. Her eyes watched his every move.

Beckett stood there leaning against the wall because she was sure her legs weren't going to hold her up without it. The pressure on her lip from her teeth was getting greater as he moved. Every movement flexed yet another muscle on his sculpted body. She looked at his tattoos, wanting to touch each one, to study them all.

Marco turned to look at her as she licked her lips. "Sweetheart, you all right?" Her eyes moved from his abs to his face. He saw the beautiful blush cover her. She nodded to him as he picked up the t-shirt and put it on, then the Kevlar.

"Marco?" she questioned. "Why that?"

"Precaution," he said as he strapped it on. When he finished, he put on his t-shirt and then the holster.

"No!' she shouted as she moved across the room, grabbing it from his hands. "No, not guns. No, Marco, please don't do this."

He was fast, wrapping his arm around her waist, pulling her to him. His other hand went to her neck. "Beckett, I'm just as scared as you are," he whispered. "I don't want to die. I don't want to do this, to expose myself. But it's the only way to free you." His head dipped, and his lips were on hers. "I need you to be free, Beck." When he kissed her, she dropped the holster, letting herself feel him.

Pulling back, she begged, "Please come back," with tears running down her cheeks.

He smiled, wiping them from her face. "It's just a funeral. How much trouble can I get into?"

"Plenty," she smarted, stepping back.

Marco laughed as he finished dressing. "How do I look?"

"Like you belong." Her voice cracked.

"I'll never belong. Come on. I need to go."

Together, they walked into the living room where Brick and eight other men were standing. Brick handed him two guns. "You know how to use these?"

Marco nodded as he put them in his holsters. "First thing Charlie taught me. You got the roses?"

"In the car. You ready?" Then to Beckett, he said, "There is food in the kitchen. There's a guy at the door, and one on the other side in my apartment. Do not open the door for anyone. I have a key." Then he reached behind his back and handed her a gun. "If anyone but me or Mr. Miller comes through that door, don't hesitate."

Beckett took the gun, checking the clip, then loaded it. Marco laughed when she stuffed it in her jeans. She looked at him. "You better come back."

He pulled her to him, hugging her, whispering, "You are scaring the shit out of me right now."

"Right back at you. Please come back."

"I will."

"Marco," she whispered, "I love you."

He ran his thumb along her bottom lip. "Aww, sweetheart." He gently kissed her, and then they left.

CHAPTER TEN

After arriving at the cemetery, Marco and the eight men got out of three black SUVs. He stood by the door while surrounded. "You got the roses?" he asked Brick.

Reaching behind him, he picked up the roses. "You okay?"

He laughed as he put one of the roses in his jacket. "I'm standing in a cemetery, in a city I never wanted to see again, about to attend a funeral of a man I hate. I left Beckett alone, and I'm carrying guns and wearing a Kevlar vest. Nope, not all right, but this needs to end. She needs to be free."

"For what it's worth, we've got three-quarters of the men on that list in custody."

Marco dipped his head. "It helps." Turning, he shut the door and proceeded to the empty gravesite with four men in front of him and four behind him. Stopping, he laid a black rose on his mother's grave, one on his father's, and one on his brother's. He didn't place one on the fake grave assigned to him.

He stood there looking at all the death Julian had wreaked. His eyes moved to the empty grave next to Benny's. Smiling, he said softly, "Karma is a bitch." He then moved to the side of the gravesite that wasn't occupied with chairs, making sure he stood a few feet away.

The cars started coming. Marco looked at the five black SUVs filled with men. He knew there were at least four snipers stationed around the cemetery. If he was going to make these people believe he was here to claim his right as the head of the family, it had to look good.

He stood there motionless, watching as they carried the casket. He knew four of the six men. They all had eyes on him. Marco tried not to smile; he knew they were unnerved by him. The chairs filled up, and there were even people standing.

Marco turned his head to speak to one of the men. "The whole family is here." The guy nodded.

The service was short, and as the priest was ending his prayer, Marco pulled the black rose from his pocket. Stepping to the coffin, he noticed all eyes were on him. Everyone was wondering who he was.

When the priest said Amen, Marco laid the black rose on the coffin, saying, "Karma's a bitch, brother." Looking at the people, he nodded and smiled. Turning, he looked at the eight men and nodded. As he moved away from the crowd, he could hear the murmurs and whispers.

As he stepped off the grass onto the drive, he heard someone say, "Excuse me." A man appeared in front of him. Marco knew who he was, his childhood friend Eric Banner. "Do I know you?" he asked.

Marco stood there looking at him for a few minutes, wondering if he should expose himself. Deciding that it wasn't the right time, he simply said, "Not anymore. Please excuse me." Stepping around him, he moved to the car. When he got in, Brick was on the phone.

"Every one of them. Yep." Then he disconnected the call, looking at Marco. "I'm just curious, why no rose for the grave of Marco Lucian?"

He laughed. "Because he's not dead anymore. Let's get out of here. I want to get back to Beckett."

∽

Marco sat looking out the window. Everyone was watching his caravan of nondescript cars with no plates pull away. Chuckling, he said, "Well, I guess I just smacked the hornet's nest." Brick laughed. "I need a few things from you."

"Name it," Brick said.

"I need you to find someone to marry us, today. And I need you to stop at a jewelry store."

"You're going to marry her?"

"If I'm going to be Marco Lucian, she needs to be protected, and the only way to make sure she's protected is if she's my wife. The family wouldn't dare touch her then."

"True. But will she marry you?"

Marco snorted. "I hope so."

The car pulled up to a jewelry store. After he bought the rings, they headed back to the apartment. At the door, he said to Brick, "Don't disturb us for a few hours." Walking in, he locked both doors. Beckett was nowhere to be seen, so he headed to the bedroom, where he found her sleeping in one of his t-shirts. He put the rings on the table along with the guns Brick had given him. His back was to the bed as he undressed.

"Marco?" Beckett's voice was groggy from sleep.

Smiling, he turned around. "Shh, go back to sleep." He climbed on the bed, pulling her into his arms.

Beckett giggled. "You're in bed."

He chuckled. "I am. Beck, we need to talk."

She sat up. "What happened?"

"Eric Banner might have figured out who I am. He asked if he knew me."

Beckett laughed. "No way. What did you say?"

He put his hand on her thigh, his thumb slowly rubbing the soft skin. "I just said, 'Not anymore,' and I walked away. Beck, the entire family was there, including wives and children."

"Tell me."

"Well, we got there early, and I put a black rose on my mom's, Benny's, and my father's gravestones."

She nodded. "What an immediate family member does. At your mom's, there was one on yours, then on her casket. At Benny's, one on yours, one on your mom's, then one on Benny's casket. Then at your father's, Julian put one on each of the graves, and then one on your father's casket."

Marco smiled. "I didn't put one on mine. I stood on the opposite side of his casket, then as the priest ended his final prayer, I stepped forward and put a black rose on his casket. I leaned down and said, 'Karma's a bitch, brother.' Then I left and here I am."

She smiled at him. "But why are you in bed with me and in your underwear?"

He reached up, pulling her to his chest. "Because I'm tired, and we need to talk about some things. Some very personal things." She snuggled into his side. "Beck, I know I sound like a broken record when I say this, but I need you to understand. Maybe give me some time, some understanding. For years after I left, my heart hurt with the loss of you. I would spend my nights making different plans to get you out, to bring you to me. Then when I met Katherine, everything changed for me. She filled the void in my heart that loving you left. My father was right; she was so much like you. She consumed me, and I gave her my heart that belonged to you. But I kept a piece of it from her. I didn't realize I had done that until Charlie gave me your license. It was like fireworks going off inside of me. I couldn't breathe. I sat in your room night after night just looking at you. I couldn't believe that, after all this time, you were right there in front of me." He touched her red hair. "The hair is a bit weird."

Beckett giggled. "I had to change my appearance."

"I'm still broken inside, Beck. It's going to take some more time. But now that we are doing this, I know the family has a code. If you can be patient with me, I want to know if you will marry me."

She pushed away from him. "You're serious?"

Marco couldn't contain his smile when he saw the fire in her eyes. He knew she was pissed. He nodded. "Yes."

Beckett was off the bed. "So, let me get this straight. You want to marry me so the family will leave me alone?" He nodded with a stupid smile on his face. "But you're still in love with your wife?" Again, he nodded. "Boy, you've got a lot of balls, Marco Lucian. A fantastic ego if you believe for one minute that I'm this hard up to accept a marriage proposal from you, a man in love with his dead wife. No! The answer is no," she shouted on her way out the door.

Marco chuckled; he knew right then in his heart that she was going to be his wife. She was still the tough little tomboy he fell in love with all those years ago. Picking up the ring box, he headed toward her voice.

Beckett was in the kitchen, slamming cabinet doors and talking to herself. "Fucking asshole. What the fuck? Who does he think he is? Egotistical bastard." She saw him leaning against the door frame, watching her. "You've got some nerve, Marco Lucian, thinking I would marry you, a man who doesn't or can't love me the way I want. The way I deserve!"

Marco was fast as he moved across the space, causing Beckett to cower away from him. He grabbed her arms to calm her down, and her knee came out of nowhere, connecting with his balls, as she screamed, "No!"

Marco went down as a blinding pain sliced through him. The ring box falling to the floor stopped Beckett in her tracks. Marco moaned, holding his balls, trying not to throw up. His moan brought her back. "Don't ever touch me again." She walked back to the bedroom and slammed the door. She went to lock it, but there was no lock. "Shit!" Moving to the bathroom, she slammed that door, screaming as she locked it. She slid down the door, covering her mouth as her tears came.

As the pain lessened, Marco sat up, leaning against the cabinet with a small smile on his face. It was his own fault for scaring her. Looking at the bedroom door, he shook his head. She was just as feisty now as she had been twenty years ago. He glanced at the blue velvet box on the floor, then picked it up and opened it. Taking the ring out, he slipped it on his baby finger.

Marco chuckled; he knew that Katherine was laughing wherever she was. "Kate, I need her," he whispered. He managed to stand and move to the bedroom. The bathroom door was shut, so he sat on the edge of the bed and waited.

Beckett sat on the floor, her tears now gone. He was everything she had ever wanted. She had loved him since she was a child, but he didn't love her like she wanted. He was only doing this to save her. Getting up, she washed her face. Looking at herself in the mirror, Beckett knew she didn't deserve much in her life. She was a murderer; she was looking at a dead woman. Looking at the door, she knew she had to face him.

Opening the door, she saw Marco sitting on the bed with his head hanging low. He was so beautiful. When he lifted his head, his eyes locked with hers, and she felt him through her whole body. His eyes filled with tears. "I'm so sorry I scared you, Beck. I didn't mean to do that." She didn't say anything. "I've loved you my whole life, and I'm sorry I forgot that."

Shaking her head, she told him, "Don't say that to me. If you loved me, you wouldn't have forgotten me. You would have come for me."

"You know that if I had come back for you, he would have found us and killed us both, along with any children we might have had. This is the way it was supposed to be."

"Bullshit. I didn't get a choice. You took that away from me. I wasn't meant to suffer the way I have. Don't you get it, Marco? I pushed him every time, wishing, hoping, praying the bastard would kill me. I wanted him to kill me."

Marco stood. "No! Don't say that."

"Why? I didn't matter enough to you. You just left me there, knowing what he was like." Marco took a step forward. "You ran and left me there. That's not love. And then, when something better came along, you forgot me altogether."

He took another step toward her. He watched her square her shoulders, his heart fluttering with pride.

"This isn't going to happen. I will not marry you just so the family will leave me alone. It doesn't matter anymore. I don't care if they kill me for killing him. He deserved that and more."

"I care, Beckett."

She laughed. "You don't care. You're a liar!" she screamed. "If you cared, you wouldn't have left me there. You only think you care because I'm standing in front of you. If I had stayed in that hotel instead of driving in that blizzard, you wouldn't have remembered me."

Marco took the last step toward her. He reached for her, but she backed away. He didn't stop until she was in his arms. "I'm sorry, Beck, so very sorry.

Beckett pushed on his chest, but he didn't let her go. Finally, she gave up and let him hold her while she cried. His heart hurt for all the pain she'd endured, for all the suffering she had dealt with because of Julian, because of him, because of the fucked-up life they were born into.

"Beck, neither of our lives turned out the way they should have, but we are together now. It shouldn't matter what roads we took to get here. We are here, at this crossroads, and we have the ability to end this fucking madness that has destroyed us both, that has torn us apart. Together, Beck, we need to do this together, so we can have the life we should have had all along. I love you, Beck. I will always love you. Please, beautiful, marry me."

"I can't, Marco."

"Why?"

"You said it yourself. You are still in love with your wife, with Katherine. It wouldn't be real. It would just be so the family will leave me alone."

Marco felt the tears well up in his eyes. "I'm sorry, Beck."

"Don't be, I get it. There has to be another way."

Marco stepped back. "I have an idea. We can wear the rings and just tell them you are my wife." He slipped the ring off his finger so she could see it.

He watched her eyes move down his chest to his hand. "Uh... you bought me a ring?"

"Beck, I know it should have been you. I can't change what happened over the past twenty years. I can only promise to try and make the rest of your life happy." She looked up at him, opening her mouth to say something. Marco wrapped his hand around her neck. Picking her up, he moved them to the bed. "Don't say no, Beck," he whispered, kissing her again.

"Marco," she moaned.

He knew he couldn't do this yet. He knew in his heart it would be Katherine in his head. "Not yet, Beck. Not yet." Putting his forehead on hers and his hands on her face, his voice rumbled as he told her, "I'm not ready yet, sweetheart."

"I know." Pulling herself up, she kissed him deeper. He got lost in her, and she in him.

Pulling back, his breathing hard, his eyes were on hers. "We need to stop." Beckett went to move, but he held her tight. "Beck, know that I don't want to stop, but Brick will be here soon. I sort of asked him to find someone to marry us."

Beckett couldn't contain her laughter as she pushed herself backward and fell onto the bed. "Ballsy move, Lucian." Marco was stunned. He hadn't heard her laughter in a very long time, not since they were kids. "What?" Beckett giggled.

"I just... Beck, you have such a beautiful laugh."

She sat up, getting on her knees, her fingers touching his lips. "I haven't had anything to laugh about since that day in the field. The day you died. I'll agree to pretend to be your wife, and when you're ready, if you still want me, then I'll marry you for real."

Marco grabbed her in his arms, kissing her hard. She couldn't stop giggling, which caused him to laugh. They separated, and Beckett sat back on her heels. They sat looking at each other, both of them smiling. Looking at his hand, Marco presented her with the ring. "Beckett, when we are ready, will you marry me?"

She looked at his hand, at the ring he had bought for her. "Yes, Mr. Lucian, when we are ready, I will marry you."

Marco took her hand in his, putting the ring on her finger, and then sweetly kissed her. The knock on the door broke their bubble. Marco got up and grabbed his jeans, then went to answer the door, leaving Beckett sitting on the bed, looking at the ring.

He wasn't sure how he was feeling about this turn of events. Opening the adjoining door, he saw Brick was there with another man. Smiling, Marco said, "We don't need your services. We've decided to go in a different direction."

Brick laughed. "She turned you down?"

"Not exactly. I'm still mourning the loss of my wife and children. I've got my own personal shit to deal with."

Brick thanked the man and walked him out. When he came back, he closed the door and walked into the apartment. "Mr. Miller, we've been doing some work, and we have a plan. If you and Miss Angelo would like to come over to my place, we can fill you in. We could use your input."

Marco nodded. "Let us eat and we'll be over."

Brick left as Beckett came out of the bedroom. They ate and headed next door.

Jay, Brick, Marco, and Beckett sat around the dining room table going over all the information from the journals. Brick had every page photocopied, so everyone had copies of the pages.

"Most of the heads were at the funeral," Brick said, producing photos of everyone. Beckett confirmed who each man was.

"A few of the women in these pictures are just as deadly as the men." Beckett pointed out who would pose a threat.

"So, what are you doing?" Marco asked.

Brick looked at Beckett. "How did you get out of the house without being seen?"

"In Marcel's office, there's a private bathroom. In the bathroom is a closet, and the back wall of the closet is a door. When I opened it, there was a staircase, which opened up in the garage."

Brick looked at Marco. "You still willing to play the head of the family?"

"What do you have in mind?"

Beckett stood up. "No!" she shouted. "They will kill you before you ever make it to the house." She bolted from the room, slamming the door behind her.

Marco smiled. "She is very adamant concerning my role in all of this. She has a great deal of information stored in that stubborn head of hers." He looked at Brick. "What's the plan?"

"Well, Jay, Mr. Adams, and I have been recruiting, so to speak. We have about thirty men so far, with no connections to any of the names on your list. We are ready to move in and replace the men on the Lucian compound. Once we have quietly replaced them, you should be safe there." Marco swallowed hard. He wasn't sure he could go back there. "Once you make yourself known, the heads of the families will come to talk. One by one, we will take them down."

"You do realize that each one of them is never without guards."

"We know. We are still recruiting more men."

"This sounds like a good plan. But is there enough evidence to arrest and convict them all?"

"I believe your father provided more than enough proof."

"But can you make it stick? Can you take them all down?"

Brick nodded. "We need to get into the house to check things out. That's where Beckett comes in since she knows where things are. Do you think she'd be willing to talk to us? I know she's pretty upset."

Marco chuckled. "She'll help. She's scared, but who can blame her? Get it together. I'm in. I want this over. The sooner the better." Marco stood. "I'll be back.

∾

Marco stood leaning against the doorframe of the bedroom with his arms crossed. Beckett was sitting against the headboard with her legs pulled up to her chest. Looking up, her eyes locked with his. He smiled at her. "You haven't changed one bit." He moved toward her. "Still as feisty as you were when we were kids." He climbed on the bed, sitting next to her. "It's a solid plan, Beck."

"No, Marco, it's not. Do you really think they give a shit if you die in the process?"

"I won't let that happen."

"You aren't bulletproof," she smarted.

"No, but with your expertise and the fact that I have no desire to die anytime soon, I think we'll be fine."

"You are so sure of yourself."

"No, Beck, I'm not. I'm scared shitless. I don't want to do this."

"Then don't. Marco, we can take the money and disappear."

"Beck, I'm not going to live my life looking over my shoulder. I want to go home. I have a good life there, an honest life, and I'd like to share it with you."

"Yeah?"

He chuckled. "Yes, now come on. The sooner we do this, the sooner we can go on that vacation."

"Fine, but I'm going on the record here, saying that this is a bad idea."

"Noted." Marco got up, putting his hand out, waiting for her to get up and take it.

Back in Brick's apartment, Beckett told them all about the guards at the house, the security room, and everything else she could remember.

"Well, I think we can do this. Miss Angelo, do you know the code to the front gate?" Beckett gave it to him. "Why don't the two of you get some rest? We should have the house and property cleared by morning." Looking at Marco, he smiled. "Then the games can begin."

CHAPTER ELEVEN

Marco woke with the now familiar feeling of warmth that radiated from deep within him. Her scent was so different from Katherine's. He knew he loved the woman in his arms, and he knew, no matter the cost, he would spend his life with her.

Moving his hand up her side, his thumb brushed gently over her already taut nipple. Marco moaned as Beckett tilted her head up. "What are you doing?" she whispered in a sleepy voice.

"What feels natural," he moaned as her knee applied pressure to his balls. Marco moved his hand into her hair and kissed her. Somehow, he maneuvered her until she was on top of him.

"Marco," she moaned deeply when she felt him against her leg.

He let himself feel her. He let his mind go as his emotions took control. His heart started beating again, filling with the love he had forgotten, the love she deserved from him. The love he could never show her or give her. Slowing the kiss, he pulled her head back. "Beck, we need to stop. I want you, beautiful, but I need to be sure it's you in my heart."

She smiled at him. "Oh, you know, Marco. You're just scared, but you know, and I know that you know."

He chuckled. "Oh yeah? Care to tell me how you think you know?"

Licking her lips, she kissed him again, then pushed herself up. "By the way you just kissed me. I felt the change in you. It's okay because I'm not ready yet either. But we'll get there. I'm going to take a shower. Care to join me?"

Marco chuckled. "You go on, sweetheart. It's not time yet." He watched her walk through the bedroom door as he adjusted himself.

Brick knocked on the door, and Marco answered. "We've secured the house. My men are all in place."

"Beckett is coming with us. I need you to clean up my father's office. That's where it happened. Oh, can you get my father's medical records? Julian poisoned him; it should be in there. We should be ready in about an hour. Get your warrants; we'll take them one at a time."

"Already have the warrants. You sure you want to do this?"

"I want her free of this. The only way is to take this family apart. Brick, I'm trusting you to do right by both of us. You said she walks if I do this. I'd like that in writing before we leave here."

Brick nodded as he left. Marco closed the door and then rested his forehead on it. "Fuck." He never wanted to see that house again. It was filled with nothing but the horrors of a childhood he didn't want to remember. He knew he needed to be strong. If he showed the slightest bit of fear, he'd be dead before he hit the floor. He felt her before she moved between him and the door. Her tiny hands came to rest on his chest just as he opened his eyes.

"Hey, you okay?"

He smiled. "Not really. Beck, I don't think I've ever been this scared."

"Even when Julian nearly killed you?"

"Back then, I welcomed it. I wanted him to kill me. At least then, the pain and suffering would have ended. Hell, Beck, a month ago, I would have welcomed a death sentence."

"And now?"

He raised his hand off the door and touched her face. "Now, I have you back in my life. Something I dreamed of for ten years."

"Until..."

He chuckled. "Yeah, until. Beck, I can't do this without you. I can't walk out that door and leave you here alone. Will you come with me? Will you do this with me?"

"I don't want to go back there. But yes, Marco, I'll go with you. I don't want to be left again. If we are going to die, we are going to do it together."

He was quick, grabbing her legs and lifting her. His mouth covered hers. "We aren't going to die." They stood there kissing with Beckett wrapped around him, his hand in her hair, holding her face. Pulling back, Marco looked at her swollen lips. "God, Beck, you are so beautiful."

The knocking brought a smile to both of their faces. Marco whispered to her, "I'll be glad when there will be no one to interrupt us."

Beckett giggled as he slid her down his body. "Oh my!" she moaned as her core felt his erection.

Laughing, Marco stepped back so she could move. Opening the door, Brick nodded. "We're ready." He handed Marco a petite Kevlar vest. "For Miss Angelo."

Marco nodded at him. "Give us a few."

Closing the door, they went to finish dressing. "Brick gave this to me for you. I need you to wear it." Not saying a word, Beckett took it.

As the six black SUVs traveled in formation through the streets of Chicago, Marco and Beckett sat in the back seat holding hands. The closer they got to the house, the greater the fear and panic consumed them both.

Marco felt as if they were walking into an unforgivable situation out of the *Godfather* movies. Looking out the window as they turned off the highway, he knew it was a matter of minutes before every fear he'd ever experienced as a child would be right in front of him. He felt Beckett squeeze his hand, causing him to look at her. "I'm scared," she whispered.

"Me too," he whispered back.

They pulled up to the gate, as it opened, Marco noticed there were men everywhere with automatic weapons. "Jesus, Brick."

"We are eighty-five strong, all with orders to shoot to kill. This ends here."

Marco wasn't convinced. No one ever really survived the family. He knew, eventually, everything caught up to you. Hell, he was living proof of that. He squeezed Beckett's hand as they pulled up to the front of the house. "Can we have a minute?" Brick and the driver got out, shutting the doors. Marco turned to look at Beckett. "Before we get out of this car and paint an even bigger target on our backs, I need to say this to you, Beck. My whole life here, you were my friend, but somewhere things changed between us. You've been in my heart for all of my life. I need you... No, I want you to know that I love you. I've always loved you. I am going to fight to the death if I have to."

He watched her eyes fill with tears, her hand moving up to touch his face. "Don't leave me."

"I won't, sweetheart. I promise." His voice filled with emotion. "I won't," he whispered on her lips. "You ready?" She shook her head. "Wait for me. If we are being watched, this needs to look like you are my wife." Marco got out of the car, then after walking around to the other side, he opened Beckett's door and helped her out. Taking her hand, they moved as one to the house. When the door opened, Marco stopped. His heart stopped as his mind filled with a rush of memories.

"You okay?" Beckett asked.

"Not sure." His voice came out soft. "I just never thought I would ever walk through these doors again. Beck, I'm not sure I can do this."

"Marco," she moved to stand in front of him, "look at me." His eyes moved to hers. "We don't have to do this. They have everything they need to take the family down. We are decoys. We are the easy way out for them."

"I want this over with. I don't want us living our lives on the run, always moving, always looking over our shoulders."

She nodded, moving out of his way. Marco forced himself to move. Crossing over the threshold was like stepping back in time. Every room had a memory, and none of them were pleasant or good.

His eyes scanned the stairs, all the way to the top. He noticed the walls were bare, Julian's doing he was sure. His feet continued to move, Beckett by his side as they started down the hallway. He stopped outside the closed ornate oak door—his father's office. He felt Beckett's grip on his hand tighten. Turning his head, he reached up to touch her face. "I had them clean it up." She nodded, looking at him. Marco leaned in, kissing her on the forehead. "I'm terrified, Beck."

"No more than I."

Marco reached for the handle, his hand shaking. Beckett put her hand on top of his, and together they opened the door. He could remember all the times he was called to this very room. Each time, he left bruised and bloody. For Beckett, it was worse. She had murdered Julian in this room. He stepped forward, stopping as a memory filled his mind.

"You wanted to see me, Father?"

"Shut the door," his father yelled.

Marco was shaking, just thirteen years old, as he closed the door. He felt his father grab him by the back of the neck and push him into the room. Marco slammed to the floor on his hands and knees.

His eyes looked at the exact spot.

His father's foot connected with his ass, pushing him into the front of his desk, cutting his face, just above his left eyebrow. "Your teacher called with your final grades. I am not raising a fucking stupid child," he screamed at him. "Get up, you little fuck." Marco stood, and when he turned to face his father, the slap across his head knocked him to the floor and left his ear ringing.

"Marco?" Beckett's voiced pulled him back. "Hey, look at me." He turned his head, tears dripping onto his cheeks. She wrapped her arms around him. "I'm here."

"Why couldn't he love me like a real father?"

"I don't know, but he can't hurt you anymore. He gave us the power to end this. So, let's end it because I really would like to take that vacation you talked about."

He chuckled. "Me too." Pulling back, he touched her face. "Thank you."

Brick appeared behind Beckett. "You all right?"

Marco nodded. "It's been a long time. Just dealing with some ghosts. We'll be all right. Can you give us some time?"

"Sure, just let me know." He reached for the door, pulling it closed behind him. "I'll be out here."

They stood there looking at each other. Beckett smiled a small smile. "This house doesn't only hold horrors. We had some good times here as well when we were kids. I always found solace in the kitchen. Remember how we used to sneak in there and steal cookies, and Cook would chase us out?"

He chuckled. "Yeah, I remember."

"Marco, we can just focus on the good memories. Let the ghosts go. We can't change the past."

"No, we can't. Let's get it done." He reached around her to open the door when Beckett stopped him.

"Wait." She moved around him.

Marco turned to watch her move across the room. "What?"

"When I stabbed Julian, he knocked me on the floor and then tried to choke me. After he collapsed on top of me, I struggled to push him off. It was only a flash, but..." She knelt in front of the desk. "I saw something. It bothered me for a few minutes, but with trying to escape and all, I let it..." She got really quiet. "Marco, look." Her voice was soft yet excited.

He moved to where she was and crouched down. He asked, "What are you looking at?"

She pointed. "That."

His eyes followed her finger, but he didn't see anything. "Beck, I don't see anything." She giggled as she lay on her back, scooting under the desk. "What are you doing?"

"This." He watched as her fingers touched the left side of the desk. "It's the slightest imperfection in the wood. You would think that, as much as this desk cost, it would be perfect."

He watched as her fingers ran across the slight rise in the wood. "Is it a switch?"

"No, it's smooth. "She pulled herself all the way through and stood

149

up behind the desk, then sat down in the chair, giggling. "Well, this feels weird. You ready?"

He stood, laughing. "For what?" He could see the mischief in her eyes as they danced. His heart warmed more at the memories of her as a child, and the great adventures they had as children.

Her eyebrows raised. "To push it." Her hand moved under the desk. "Ready?"

His smile said it all as she pushed the imperfection. They both heard a click. Marco saw the bookcase behind her move just the slightest bit. "Son of a bitch." He moved behind the desk as Beckett stood up.

"What is it?" Pulling on the bookcase, it swung open. "Holy shit," Beckett whispered. On the wall was a map of sorts, of names. "It's the family."

They stood there reading the names. Looking down, Beckett saw an envelope sitting on the edge. She tapped his arm. "Look."

Marco looked down. Picking it up, he saw his name was on it. Turning it over, he opened it. "How did he know I would find this?" She shrugged her shoulders. Opening the letter, he walked over to the chair and sat down. Beckett stood looking at all the names.

Marco,

I always knew you were the smart one. As you can see by the wall, I've listed everyone involved. Start at the top and work your way down the list.

There are three men who are not on any payroll I could find: Jay Munch, who is in fact Charlie's wife's cousin, Allen Brick, and James Adams.

These men have been trying for years to take us apart, but I managed to convince Joey Malone to insert himself into Munch's life, so we've always been a step ahead.

Well, here is my payback for all the wrong I've done. Take each Don and his Capos one at a time. Be quick, so it's not too noticeable.

Years ago, when I realized that Julian was poisoning me, I sent him on a business trip. While he was gone, I had a secure room built under the house. It's a keypad lock, and the combo is your birthdate, year included. Use it to stash them until you have them all. If the press gets wind of the disappearances, everyone will scatter.

Now, if by chance you decide to take over, then the list is to show you who you will need to dominate. I am hoping Charlie did a better job of raising you into a man and you don't want this.

In the bathroom, in the closet is a door, leading down a staircase to the garage. Instead of opening the door on the right, turn left and face the wall. Push on the left-hand side of the wall about chest high, and a panel will pop open to expose the keypad.

Get in touch with Jones. He will help you deal with getting the family here. In the bottom drawer on the left-hand side, take everything out and press on the bottom of the drawer. There is a hidden compartment that holds a file. Give it to Jones. He will know what to do with it.

In the end, Marco, you will own everything that I own. Do with it what you want. Burn the place to the ground, son, if it makes up for every wrong thing I've done to you.

Remember, no matter what you think of me or feel for me, I have loved you your whole life.

Good luck, son, in whatever path you choose. I can only hope and pray it is the right one.

Your father

Marco picked his head up. Beckett was standing at the desk looking at him. He smiled at her. "We are going on that vacation."

"Why, what does it say?"

He got up and handed her the letter, then went to the door. "Brick, can I see you?" He walked in, and Marco locked the door, "I need you to get Jones here. He is going to help us."

Brick nodded, looking at the open bookcase. "What's all this?"

"It's our road map to end this, courtesy of Marcel Lucian."

Brick moved closer. "Son of a bitch," he mumbled as he read the names. "How did you know it was here?"

Marco was watching Beckett. Her eyes moved from the letter to him. She smiled a small smile. "I saw the lever when Julian fell on me." Her eyes moved to the bathroom, then back to Marco. He nodded.

Beckett showed them how to gain access to the staircase. Her bloody clothes were still on the stairs where she left them. "No one knows this is here," she said, touching Marco's arm.

"How do you know?"

"Look." She pointed to her bloody clothes. "That's what I was wearing when I stabbed Julian."

Marco moved around her and picked up the blood-stained clothes. "Come on, sweetheart, let's see what sick shit the old man was up to."

The three of them moved down the stairs, and Marco did what his father told him. After entering the code, the door popped open. Pushing on it, they found that the room was vast, filled with chairs. Marco chuckled. "How could he have known any of this would happen?"

"Maybe he hoped," Beckett said softly.

Looking at Brick, he stated, "I hope you have enough handcuffs."

He laughed. Marco closed up the room, and they headed back upstairs. "Brick, you need to get Jones here before we begin this. He knew where I was, who I was."

"He'll be here this evening. When do you want to start this?"

"I need to speak to Jones, so maybe tomorrow would be good. If we do this right, we can end it all in a week."

Brick moved to the door. "The house is secure. I had one of the guys bring your bags in, and they're in the front hall." He walked out leaving Marco and Beckett alone.

～

"This is fucked up, Beck."

"Tell me about it. It's the end, Marco. Hopefully, it will go smoothly."

Pulling her to him, he kissed her forehead. "You know it's not going to happen that way."

"I know, but a girl can dream."

He chuckled. "You hungry?"

"Yes, but I could use a drink. Doesn't your father have a secret stash of scotch around here?"

"As a matter of fact." He let go of her, moving toward the desk, where he opened the bottom drawer and pulled out a bottle. "My father had a glass every night." Setting the bottle on the desk, he just stood there looking at it. "In his letters, he said Julian was poisoning him." His eyes moved to Beckett's. "I'll bet you it's in the scotch."

"You think?"

"Pretty sure. It would be the only thing that was a constant with my father. Did Brick say if he was leaving?"

"I don't know. I'll check."

A few minutes later, Brick walked in. "Miss Angelo said you wanted to see me. She told me to let you know she's in the kitchen getting food."

Marco started to panic. He told Brick as he started out of the room, "That bottle of scotch, have it tested. My father was poisoned by Julian. I think that's how he did it." As he moved through the house, his heart pounded in his chest as he neared the kitchen, he heard voices.

"How did you get in here?" Beckett asked.

"The guard let me in," the man responded.

"Eric, what are you doing? Let me go."

Marco pulled out one of his guns, clicking off the safety. "I don't know what you're trying to do here, Beckett, but Mr. Romano wants to see you. So, if I were you, I wouldn't make a scene. Come on, let's go."

Marco listened to him laugh as he crossed the threshold. The man had Beckett pinned against the refrigerator. Putting the gun to the man's head, he pulled back the hammer. "I suggest you let my wife go, or the housekeeper is going to be cleaning your brains off the wall." He let her go. "Beck, go get our friend. I left him in my office." To the man, he said, "Why don't you sit down and make yourself comfortable."

The man moved to the table. Marco kept the gun pressed to his head while he sat down. "Now put your weapons on the table."

"Who are you?" the man asked while he placed a gun and two knives on the table.

Brick came running in. "What's going on?" He looked at the man.

"This gentleman here thought it was acceptable to touch my wife."

Marco smiled at Beckett, whose eyes were dancing. "Sweetheart, did he hurt you?"

Smiling, she shook her head. "No, but he said Mr. Romano wanted to see me."

"Is that right?" Brick handcuffed him to the chair and picked up his knives and gun. Marco released the hammer and holstered his gun. Pulling out the ring he bought himself, he slipped it on his finger. He handed Beckett the matching one, then moved around the table to look at the man, letting him see his face. He had to hide his chuckle.

"You're the guy from the funeral. Who are you?"

"I should be disappointed that you don't remember me, Eric. What the hell happened to you that you are now a thug for Romano?"

"That's none of your business. They want Beckett for killing Julian Lucian."

Marco laughed. "Beckett is my wife. No one touches her. She didn't kill Julian, I did. Well, he had a heart attack, actually, when I went to see him."

Eric sat there looking at him. "The only two people who went into his room were that fucking F.B.I. pussy, Munch, and one of his goons."

Marco put his hand up, chuckling. "I'm that goon." Jay walked into the room. "Hey, Jay, did you know you were a pussy?"

"Nope, never tried it." He laughed. "Mr. Banner, what brings you by the house? Doing some dirty work for Romano?"

Eric was looking at Marco. "Who are you?"

"You haven't told him yet?" Jay asked Marco.

Marco looked at Eric. "Not yet. I was waiting for him to connect the dots. But I guess it's just like math class. He could never figure out the word problems; he always copied off my paper."

Beckett giggled when Eric turned ashen. "No fucking way."

"Oh, so you finally admit you cheated?"

"This is a dangerous game you are playing. Marco Lucian died twenty years ago. I was at his funeral."

"Well, Eric, here's the thing. That coffin is empty. They never found a body because there wasn't one to find."

Eric laughed. "You're a dead man. Romano won't accept this; he is making a move to take over."

"Well then, when he gets here tomorrow, I guess I'm going to have to tell him the position is filled."

"By whom? You? You won't last a..."

Marco watched him process what had happened. "I see you're still not the sharpest crayon in the box. I work for the F.B.I., Eric. The family is done. I'm here to take my place as the head of this family, along with my wife. My father left me everything I need, and you, my old friend, are my first guest. Mr. Brick, would you please escort Mr. Banner out of here? My wife and I would like to eat." Marco winked at Beckett. "Has Mr. Jones arrived yet?"

"He's about twenty minutes out," Jay answered as he shoved Eric.

"Oh, one of your guys at the gate let him in. I'd check into that. I really don't want to get blood all over the house. We have a busy week."

Brick busted out laughing as Marco pulled Beckett to his chest. "Jesus, Beck, I was so scared. Don't leave me again. I can't keep you safe if you aren't with me."

"I know, I'm sorry. Brick said the house was secure."

Leaning in, Marco kissed her temple, whispering, "I don't trust any of these guys. I trust you, Beck."

"I was going to make us sandwiches."

He let her go, and the two of them ate. After, Marco grabbed their bags, and they went back into the office. "This is the only room we are staying in. We have a bathroom and a way out. The door locks, so we'll stay in here until it's over. I'll have one of them get us some pillows and blankets."

Beckett smiled at him. "Marco, can we really do this and survive?"

"I don't know, but I'm hopeful."

"Oh, that's encouraging."

He laughed. "Hey, I'm trying to be optimistic. Beck, I don't think we survived twenty years to not make it out of this alive."

～

Brick opened the door. Being a smart ass, he said, "Mr. Jones to see Mr. Lucian."

Marco chuckled. "Mr. Miller," he said as Jones walked into the room handcuffed. "Mr. Jones, I believe it's time for you to atone for your sins. Come on in and have a seat. There are plans to make and deals to be made."

Jones stood there looking at him, then at Beckett. "Miss Angelo, the family is not happy about you killing Julian. They are looking for you."

She smiled at him. "I'm pretty sure they know where I am."

Marco smiled at her. "Miss Angelo is under my protection. The family will not touch her."

Jones looked at him. "And who are you?"

Marco laughed. "Oh, Mr. Jones, you thought you were going to take my place as the head of this family."

"There is no head of this family, not since Miss Angelo murdered him."

"Well, you see, Mr. Jones, Beckett didn't kill my brother. He had a heart attack when I went to see him. He knew, if he ever walked out of that hospital, he was a dead man. Beckett is married to me now, so she is under my protection."

"Your brother?" Jones stood there looking at him.

Marco smiled. "Mr. Jones, you know who I am. Why else would you want Joey to kill me?"

Jones swallowed hard. "Marco?" He choked on his name. His eyes moved to Beckett. "You married him?" She nodded. "But you were supposed to marry Julian."

"No, that's what Julian told everyone. Marcel never intended for it to happen. I was always to be Marco's wife."

"But he's married to someone else," Jones sputtered out.

Marco could see the confusion and fear in his eyes. He knew something wasn't right here. Shaking his head, he said, "You know what happened to my family. Now, you are going to help us take this family apart, starting with Romano."

Jones shook his head. "It's a death sentence."

Beckett pulled the gun from her jeans. "The way I see it, you know everything. You even know where the bodies are buried and who buried them. I've already murdered Julian to escape this fucking insanity. I don't have a problem taking you out as well. Because, Mr. Jones, I have full immunity by helping them end this family. So, really, what's another body? It's nothing compared to the bodies that are going to be stacking up."

Brick and Jay stood by the door, trying not to smile like fools.

"What's in it for me?" he asked.

Marco leaned over, looking at Brick, and said, "Depends on what you have to offer and how well you play your part." Jones sat there for a long time. No one moved. No one spoke. Beckett was watching Jones; she had spent years watching people. She knew he was full of shit. There was something else going on. Something more. Jones moved his eyes to Beckett; he knew this woman would destroy everyone in her path. "Fine, I'll help." She knew he was lying.

"Well, Mr. Jones, it's time to make things right," Marco said to him, then looked at Brick. "Take him someplace and record what he has to say. Beckett and I need to talk." Jones' eyes never left Beckett's. She knew he was lying. He wasn't going to help. It was just the opposite.

When Brick shut the door, she walked over, locking it. Taking Marco's hand, she led him to the bathroom. She turned on the shower, opened the closet, released the latch, and led him into the stairwell. "Marco, he's lying. Something's not right here. How did Eric get in here? No one should have gotten past Brick's men."

"I was thinking the same thing. Are we missing something?"

"I'm not sure. Maybe we should get the file and see what it says."

"Beck, I don't have a good feeling about any of this." He kissed her forehead. Together, they went back into the room. Quietly, Marco got the file, and as he was closing the drawer, there was a knock on the door. Picking up the file, he slipped it into the back of his jeans while Beckett opened the door. Jay smiled at her.

"I figured you would want a few pillows and blankets." His eyes were on Marco. Handing the blankets to Beckett, he pushed a piece of paper in her hand as she took them from him. "Thank you," she said.

"We are just going to crash. Can you tell Brick we'll see him in a few hours?"

"You two get some sleep." Jay's eyes never left Marco's. He nodded, then turned, leaving the room.

Beckett locked the door, put the blankets and pillows on the couch, and then moved to where Marco was leaning on the desk and handed him the note. Opening it, he read the words.

This room is wired, so be careful what you say. Brick is in this up to his eyeballs. We need to get the two of you out of here. Your bags have been tagged. Sit tight. I have a plan.

Marco looked at Beckett. She took the note and slipped it into her bra. Marco pulled the file from his jeans. "Come on, sweetheart. Let's get some sleep."

They sat on the couch. Marco opened the file and began reading. As he turned the last page, Beckett got up, grabbing a pen.

What the hell are we going to do?

We need to get out of here. I'm sorry, Beck.

Don't be. If we hadn't come here, we wouldn't have known any of this.

True. Remember how we used to sneak out past the guards?

She nodded, smiling at the memory of all the times they had snuck out.

Let's wait for dark. They will be more relaxed.

Agreed. Should we check the bags?

Marco nodded. When they were finished, they found eight trackers and a few listening devices. Marco took a few pictures and sent them to Charlie.

Look familiar?

Looking at his phone, he popped the back off it. Removing the battery, he showed it to Becket. She tapped him on the chest, hitting his Kevlar. Quickly, they took them off, along with the clothes they were wearing. After they changed, Marco felt his phone vibrate.

They sure do. Everything all right?

Nope. I'll be in touch.

Marco showed Beckett Charlie's number, touching his head for her to remember it. He nodded, then snapped his phone in half and stuffed it down in the back of the couch. They sat there until the room grew dark. Checking the time, Marco nodded to her. They took the cash out of the bag, putting it in the black shirt. Marco tied it to Beckett, under her shirt. He took the file, the letters, and the envelopes from his father, doing the same thing around him. Together, they made their way down the hidden staircase to the garage. Beckett had memorized where the cameras were around the compound, and she knew all of the blind spots.

The excitement they both felt overrode the fear, just like when they were children. Together, holding hands, they maneuvered through the blind spots into the tree line at the back of the house. Marco remembered the path they took as children to the back wall surrounding the property, right to the loose stones. Once they were out of the compound, Beckett led them to her family home and into the garage, where she grabbed the keys to her car, and together they disappeared into the night.

CHAPTER TWELVE

As they drove across the country, only stopping to change cars, Marco drove while Beckett slept, then Beckett drove while he slept.

They dumped the last car deep in the woods and hitchhiked the rest of the way. Marco knew it was stupid to go home, but it was the only place he could think of where he felt safest.

They didn't talk while they traveled the roads, and it was late when the last truck driver dropped them a mile outside of town. As he pulled away, Marco and Beckett disappeared into the woods. The snow was nearly thigh-high for Beckett. They were nearly freezing by the time they reached Charlie's house. As they moved into the back-yard, a light turned on upstairs.

Marco knocked lightly on the back door and smiled at Beckett. They could finally eat a hot meal and get into some warm, dry clothes.

When the porch light came on, Marco moved them against the wall. The light went off, and he reached over, gently knocking again. When the door opened, he stepped in front of it with his finger to his lips.

Charlie grabbed him into a bear hug. Once in the house, Beckett made a gesture of writing. While they took off their boots and gear, Charlie handed Marco a pen and paper.

Don't turn on the lights. We need dry clothes. Beckett is freezing.

He handed Charlie the paper.

Go to the basement.

Marco read the note, then after taking Beckett's freezing hand, they followed Charlie. He opened a door off the kitchen and then disappeared. Marco and Beckett went down the stairs. He pulled her to his chest; she was shaking.

Charlie and Elizabeth came down the stairs. He touched Marco on the shoulder, gesturing for them to follow him. He walked them across the basement, into a smaller room. It was so dark Marco could barely see in front of him. Elizabeth pulled the door closed, plunging them into complete darkness.

Charlie clicked on a flashlight and stepped to a side wall, where he moved a few cans on a shelving unit. Marco heard a series of clicks. Beckett squeezed his hand as he watched Charlie turn, shining the light on the wall to his left. Marco followed him with Beckett in tow. Pushing on the wall, it opened into another room. They all moved inside, and Charlie pushed the door shut. He went to talk, and Marco shook his head, nodding to the clothes Elizabeth was holding.

They changed, handing everything to Elizabeth. Charlie opened the door, putting the clothes outside. When the door closed, Beckett burst into tears, sobbing while Marco held on to her.

"What happened?" Charlie asked.

Elizabeth grabbed a blanket off the bed, wrapping it around Beckett. "She's freezing. Her lips are purple." Turning away, she turned on the heaters. "Come over here, dear. Sit by the heater."

Marco let her go, looking at Charlie. "We were played. Jay warned us, but we had already figured it out. We got out of there right after I sent you that text. We drove and then hitch-hiked. We've been walking through the woods for the past few hours."

"You're safe here. Liz, why don't you get them some hot tea?"

"It's fine. We just need to sleep for a while. You guys go back to bed. Charlie, can you burn those clothes and our coats?"

Elizabeth smiled, touching Marco's arm. "There is a bathroom right there. You stay here and sleep." She looked at Beckett. "Get her warm. When you are ready to eat, just flip this switch, and the phone will ring once upstairs. Marc, don't come out of this room. Charlie had it built just for this. You are safe here. Now, come on, Charlie. Let's leave them alone."

Marco hugged her. "Thank you." He watched them leave. After pushing the door shut, his eyes moved to Beckett. "Come on, sweetheart. Let's get these clothes off and get under all these blankets."

Beckett didn't argue. She was so cold her body was shaking. Marco put all the blankets on the bed, then climbed in. When Beckett got in, Marco hissed when her ice-cold skin touched him. "Jesus, Beck. Come here." He wrapped himself around her. "God, sweetheart. You're so cold."

"D-d-don't let-t-t me go," she stuttered.

"Never." He tucked the covers around them and they crashed.

Beckett woke him when she moved away from him. "What's wrong?"

"I need to use the bathroom. Go back to sleep."

Marco watched her walk to the bathroom, his heart speeding up. When she came out, she crawled back into bed, snuggling into his side. "Thank you," she whispered.

Wrapping his arms around her, he kissed her forehead. "For what?"

"Mmm... for getting us here safely. For keeping me warm."

Marco didn't say anything, he just held her close and went back to sleep. Hours later, he woke up, still wrapped around her. This was where he belonged. It's where he had always belonged. Getting up, he used the bathroom. When he walked out, Beckett was sitting on the bed with a t-shirt on. "Put some clothes on, Marco," she said shyly.

He chuckled. "Worried about my virtue?" he smarted as he grabbed the clothes Elizabeth had given him.

She laughed. "Nope, not yours. But we need to talk about all of this. Who would we even give this information to? How are we ever going to end this? Marco, we can't live like this."

He sat in the chair and picked up the file. "I don't know, Beck. Why don't we just give it a few days? We need to eat and sleep. Neither of us has slept right in a long time. We certainly haven't eaten much. So, why don't we just relax for a few days, sharpen our brains, and get our strength back?" He looked up at her. "What's wrong?"

She smiled. "You slept in the bed with me, nearly naked."

Standing, he dropped the file on the chair. Crawling up the bed, he whispered, "I did. You were freezing, Beck. I needed to keep you warm." His lips nearly touched hers.

"Thank you." Her breath was warm on his lips.

Marco wrapped his hand around her neck, sweetly kissing her. It was the grumbling coming from her stomach that had them both laughing. "We need to eat."

He went to move, but Beckett grabbed his shirt, kissing him again. "Get me food."

Marco laughed, grabbing her. He flipped her onto her back, making her squeal, and she busted out laughing. "God, Beck, you are so beautiful."

"Food! I need food." She giggled.

Marco let her go and went to flip the switch. "Now we wait." Picking up the file, he got back on the bed. "Time to figure this out and figure out where we go from here." They sat there for what felt like hours.

Beckett looked at the door. "I hope everything is all right."

"What do you mean?"

"It's been a long time since you flipped that switch. Maybe you should flip it again. I mean, what if Elizabeth was out shopping or something?"

Marco got up and flipped the switch. When he turned around, Beckett was checking the guns. "What are you doing?"

"Something's wrong." He watched her pull the clips from his guns, popping a bullet from each one, then putting them back in. When she did the same to hers, he heard her say, "Son of a bitch."

"What?" He moved over to the bed.

"Mine has blanks in it. What the hell?"

"Here, take one of mine."

"Marco, what are you doing?"

"We are going to make sure Elizabeth and Charlie are all right."

"Just flip the switch again."

He shook his head. "If someone is up there, it will look suspicious. We can't let anyone know we are here."

She giggled. "Oh, and going up there with guns blazing is so subtle."

He chuckled. "Not blazing, just in case. Come on. If no one is home, then we can get something to eat. Just remember to be quiet. I'm sure this house is bugged. Now, come on. I'm more than a bit worried." He put his hand out. "Don't close the door. I don't remember which cans he moved."

Beckett laughed. "I do."

Together, they slowly made their way up the stairs. When he cracked the door, he heard voices. Beckett pulled the gun from her pants pocket.

"Charlie, are you sure you haven't heard from them?" Jay's voiced boomed.

"I told you, Jay. I got a picture text of trackers from him. He said he would be in touch. That was four days ago. You reassured us they would be safe. Jay, that boy is like a son to us."

"I know. I just didn't know that my boss was the one trying for the head of the family."

"Well, how did you figure that out?"

"One of Romano's guys got in the house. When Brick found out, he put a bullet in his head. I heard him tell one of his men to drop the body off at the front gate of Romano's place."

"Well, can't you do something to stop him?"

"I don't have any proof. If you hear from them, please tell him to get in touch with me. I need their help to stop this. Beckett knows so much. Maybe she heard a conversation or something."

"Why can't you go to the higher-ups?"

"It's suicide if I go without any evidence. Listen, I need to get back. Brick sent me here to see if they came back."

"Did you check the cabin?"

"Yeah, and his house. They just disappeared. Brick has a country-wide search for them."

"Wouldn't that be stupid of him if his plan is to use Marco to take out the big players?"

"That's what I said, but he's pissed that they got away from him." Jay stood up. "I'll call you in a few days. I'll figure something out. Watch the news."

"Jay, what about all the information in those ledgers? I thought that was more than enough information to dismantle the family. The only thing Marco wanted was to free Beckett."

"I know. I'll do my best, but Beckett's memory is all I have to go on now. Brick burnt the ledgers, along with all the evidence we found at the house. He kept Beckett's bloody clothes to use as evidence against her for killing Julian." Marco heard him open the door. "I'm sorry, Elizabeth, Charlie, I made a huge mistake trusting my boss." He chuckled. "I guess Marco was right; I did get knocked off my high horse. When I finish this, if I'm still alive, I'm out."

Charlie patted him on the shoulder. "Don't you know anyone who can help?"

"I did, but they have both retired. Some crazy fuck murdered their brothers. Besides, I wouldn't even know where to find them. We'll talk soon."

Marco heard the door shut. Pushing the basement door open, Charlie looked at him, shaking his head. He stepped back, pulling the door closed as Charlie opened the back door. Jay handed him a piece of paper. "Why don't you see if you can find them. It's less suspicious. Tell them I'm looking." Charlie nodded, closing the door.

Marco and Beckett went back down to the room and closed the door. "What do you think that was about?" she asked him.

"Not sure. Let's just wait."

A few minutes later, the door clicked. Marco motioned for her to go to the bathroom. He was ready to die to save her. When Elizabeth walked in with a tray of food, he relaxed. Charlie followed her with a box of food.

"Come and eat." She smiled. "I'll go get the rest of the food while you talk."

"Thank you," Beckett said.

Marco watched her leave as Charlie pushed the door closed. "You had Elizabeth worried." He chuckled. "She thought you two died down here. You've been sleeping for sixteen hours."

"So, what did Jay have to say?" Marco asked.

"Why don't you eat, and then we'll talk. I'm going to help Liz." He popped the door and left.

Marco and Beckett sat on the bed and ate. "God, I'm starving," she said, shoving food in her mouth.

"Eat, I don't need that much. Here," he pushed some of his eggs onto her plate. "I think you need this more than me."

She giggled. "Trying to fatten me up?"

"We have no idea what is coming, and you need your strength." Beckett just smiled at him and ate everything on her plate.

The door clicked, and Charlie and Elizabeth walked in carrying boxes of food. Then Marco helped, while Elizabeth explained to Beckett everything that was in the boxes. When it was all said and done, Elizabeth left.

Marco filled Charlie in on everything that happened when they left. "We found this file that my father had hidden. We didn't tell anyone about it; we just got the hell out of there." Marco handed it to him.

Charlie sat down in the chair and started reading, while Marco and Beckett sat on the bed watching him. When he finished, Charlie looked at Marco for a long time. "This is big. Where did you get this?"

Marco nodded. "My father. What was Jay doing here?"

"He was looking for you. I got the impression there is a price on your head. What's in this file is a death sentence. Who knows you have it?"

"You. Charlie, if us being here is going to cause you problems, we can leave. We are a hundred miles from the Canadian border. I'm sure we can cross without being detected. We can disappear."

"No, and no. Jay gave me the names of some men who he knew a long time ago. He said that they would be your only hope of surviving this. I'm going to find them and go see them. You two stay here in this room. Don't come out for anything."

"Charlie, I can't let you do this. I'm not dragging you into this mess."

"Marco, you didn't drag me into anything. I could have sent you away when you first showed up here, but I'm not that kind of a man. You are the son I never had. You're a good man with a kind heart, so I'm going to find these guys and I'll do whatever I can to help you."

Marco wiped the tear off his cheek. "Thank you."

"Now, you two just relax. Catch up on your sleep. The TV works, so just stay here and let me see what I can do." He stood, and so did Marco, and Charlie wrapped him in his arms. "I never felt I had the right to say this to you because you aren't mine, but I love you, son."

Marco squeezed him a bit tighter. "I love you, too."

Charlie let him go, nodding, and then he left the room. Beckett pushed the door shut and listened to the lock engage. "You all right?" She smiled at him.

"Yeah, come and lay down with me." He put his hand out.

She laughed. "So, now you want to sleep with me? In a bed?"

He chuckled, pulling her into his arms. "Yes, I'm becoming addicted to your scent."

Beckett busted out laughing. "Sure, you are. You just want to have sex with me."

Marco wrapped his hand around her neck. "I will never just have sex with you. But one day, I hope to make love to you, and I most definitely want to fuck you into next week."

Beckett's eyes got huge. "Oh!" she squeaked out.

"Yeah," he whispered on her lips, kissing her. "Now, come and lay down with me. I need to sleep."

Charlie left them and went to his office to begin his research. Hours later, he discovered that one of the men lived only two hours from him. Deciding to just head out, he took his truck, leaving the squad car behind.

His GPS led him deep into the woods. Eventually, it dropped out, so he just followed the tracks down the road. About twenty minutes in, he saw smoke in the distance. Pulling up to a sizable log cabin, he was greeted by a black and white border collie. As he was climbing out, he heard someone whistle, and the dog took off running. Charlie was met by a man who gave the term 'Brick Wall' new meaning.

"Can I help you?" he said.

"I hope so. Are you Al Blackshaw?"

He smiled at him. "Who's asking?"

"Oh, I'm sorry, I'm Charlie Jamison. I'm the sheriff up in Bells Harbor."

"I'm Al. What brings you here?"

"Well, I was hoping to talk to you. Is there someplace we can go? Or we can get back in my truck."

"Sorry, come on in. We don't get many visitors out here." He started walking, so Charlie followed him into the house, where he met his wife. Al motioned for him to sit. "So, what brings you to my door?"

"Jay Munch."

Al sat there looking at him. His wife smiled at Charlie. "Would you like a cup of coffee?"

"That would be great, thank you. Black if you don't mind." Looking at Al, he said, "Jay suggested you might be able to help me. He said you and your brother Joe are retired. But Jay believes you two are our last resort for survival."

"Well, Charlie, we are retired. But if Jay sent you looking for us then it must be bad. Why don't you tell me just how bad it is?"

Charlie took the coffee from his wife, thanking her. He watched her leave the room while he sipped the hot liquid. He didn't say anything for a long time. "Twenty years ago, a badly beaten, destroyed young man walked into my office." Shaking his head, he chuckled. "He told me this story that was assuredly the most unbelievable tale. I sent him to the café for a meal and put him in a hotel for the night. He was bruised and broken, just a scrawny boy. Terrified. I don't think he stopped shaking the entire time he talked. That night, I spent a long time researching the story he told me. It was all true. His mother had managed to get him false papers, so I discussed it with my wife, and we made a decision to help him. We legally changed his name, and he became the son we never had. Three weeks ago, his past showed up."

"What does Jay have to do with this? He's the head of the organized crime unit in Chicago. How do you know him?"

"He's my wife's cousin. I called him to come and hear a story."

"And he sent you to me? Charlie, I don't know what you think I can do to help you."

Charlie sat there looking at Al for a long time. "I almost feel that if I say this out loud, horrible things are going to happen."

Al chuckled. "As with most things in the line of work we were in, horrible things happened. Why don't you tell me?"

Taking a deep breath, Charlie said quietly, "Allen Brick and the Lucian Crime family."

Al didn't blink, nor did he move, he just sat there looking at him for a long time. Taking a deep breath, he stood. "Would you excuse me?"

Charlie nodded. He watched Al grab what looked like a satellite phone. After kissing his wife on the forehead, he walked out the door.

"Hey, brother, what's up?" Joe answered.

Al chuckled. "You wouldn't believe me if I told you. How's Roni doing?"

"Getting bigger by the day."

"Becca is so excited; she's been doing all kinds of shopping."

"Al, what's going on?"

"Fuck, Joe. There's a man sitting in my living room looking for our help."

Joe chuckled. "We're retired. Jesus, Al, I'm about to become a father. I want no part of this."

"Yeah, I know. I wouldn't have called if I didn't think we should at least discuss this."

"That bad?"

"It's pretty bad. How about I send Becca and the animals to you, and we at least have a sit down with this guy?"

"Can you at least give me a hint?"

"Allen Brick." There was silence on the other end. "Joe?"

"Send her. I'll be there when she lands."

The line went dead. Al stood there looking at the lake. Turning, he shook his head. He was happy with the life he'd built with Becca here. He made his way back inside the house.

"Charlie, why don't you leave me a number where I can get in touch with you, and I'll call you in a day or two?"

Charlie nodded, pulling out his business card. "Thank you for listening." They shook hands and Charlie left with the hope of possible help to save them.

CHAPTER THIRTEEN

Marco smiled as he woke up, feeling Beckett tucked into his chest. He had no idea how much time had passed or if it was day or night. They ate, talked, and slept, something neither of them had done in a very long time.

He hadn't had time to let himself be absorbed with his grief. He was surviving, just like Katherine made him promise he would do. Smiling, he was pretty sure she didn't mean for him to get involved with the mob or be hiding in a safe room in Charlie's basement.

Unwrapping himself from Beckett, he grabbed some clean clothes and took a shower. He needed to shave; it had been days. When he opened the door, Beckett was still sleeping. His smile was automatic when he looked at her. Trailing his knuckles down her cheek, he watched her smile. "Hey, sweetheart."

"Mmm... Come back to bed," she mumbled.

He climbed on the bed, gently kissing her. "Come on, let's eat."

She giggled. "I don't want to get up."

Marco laughed, getting off the bed. "Come on." He put his hand out. She took it, and he pulled her up into his arms, kissing her.

"This, I could do all day."

Marco chuckled, letting her go. They ate, and then she took a shower.

He was sitting in the chair when the door clicked. Grabbing a gun, he moved to the wall as the door opened. Charlie walked in, and following behind him were two men. Charlie nodded to him. Putting the gun in his jeans, Charlie closed the door.

"This is Al and Joe Blackshaw," Charlie said.

Marco put his hand out to shake theirs. "Marc Miller." He looked at Charlie. "What's going on?"

"You need help, so I went to have a conversation with Al, and he agreed to come and have a conversation with you."

Marco motioned for them to sit and knocked on the bathroom door. "Beck, we have company." Turning, he looked at Al. "What did Charlie tell you?"

"Not much, really. He told me a story about a bruised, scared, scrawny teenager who showed up here telling him a story that scared the shit out of him. He said, for twenty years, everything was fine until this person's past walked back into his life." Beckett walked out of the bathroom, causing Al to chuckle. "I take it you are that boy, and she is your past?"

Marco chuckled. "She is part of it, yes. And I am that boy, but what I don't know is why would a story like that bring you here?"

"Well, Charlie said that Jay sent him to find me. He also mentioned my old boss, Allen Brick, and the Lucian crime family. Two things that I believe go hand in hand."

Beckett looked at Al. "You're ex F.B.I.?"

Al nodded. "It was because of Brick that I quit. I knew he was dirty then, but I had no proof."

"We tried for years to get evidence on him and his ties to organized crime," Joe added. "But it was all just speculation."

Al looked at Marco. "So, why are we here?"

Beckett looked at Marco. "I know their names. I think you should tell them. We need help. We can't live our lives like this, locked in a safe room."

"You sure?"

"We are dead either way." She touched his face.

Marco smiled at her, then turned his head and took a deep breath. "My name is Marco Lucian, and this is Beckett Angelo."

Al busted out laughing. "Marco Lucian died twenty years ago, murdered by his brother Julian." Al's eyes shifted to Beckett. "You're the one who killed Julian."

"Both of those statements are lies. My parents got me out, gave me fake papers. I've lived here for the past twenty years."

"I can prove it," Charlie said. "I have pictures of him from when he first showed up here."

"Beckett may have stabbed Julian, but he was a drug addict. He had a heart attack after I paid him a visit, letting him know I was still alive. Jay was there with me. He got me in the room."

"Let's say this is all true," Joe began. "Tell me why I left my very pregnant wife to travel across the country."

After Marco and Beckett told them everything, Marco handed Al the file. "My father left me a letter telling me where that was. I believe he wrote it just days before he died. No one knows I have it, not even Jay. We left and came back here. Brick had us wired with trackers and listening devices. This room is the only guaranteed safe place."

Al set the file down. "Charlie, do you mind if we check out your house?"

"Not at all."

Looking at Marco, he said, "We'll be back."

Beckett looked at Marco when the door shut. He wrapped his arms around her. "What's going through that head of yours?"

"I'm scared, that's all. I was enjoying being in this bubble with you."

He laughed, kissing her. "Yeah?"

Her fingers touched his lips. "Yeah."

They lay back on the bed kissing. "Marco, you feel different."

"Maybe because I am different. I know Katherine will always be a part of me, a part of who I am. But now you are becoming everything to who I am. You are an amazing woman, and every minute I spend with you makes the next one mean even more. Beck, I love you." His mouth crushed down over hers.

"I've always loved you. Spending time with the grown-up you just makes it more intense."

He laughed. "The grown-up me knows a great deal more than the teenage me you used to know."

Giggling, she sat up. "Well, considering I know factually what you are talking about, but not physically, I'll just have to take your word for it."

Marco sat up. "Hey," he whispered on her neck, "what we are going to share will be beautiful, soft, and tender. Never violent, never forced." She leaned back against his chest. Marco turned her head. "I promise, Beck. When we are ready, it will be beautiful." He gently kissed her.

The door clicking separated them. Charlie walked in. "Come on, the house is secure. You two look like you could use some sun."

Marco grabbed the file, and they followed Charlie upstairs to the dining room. He handed Al the file as they sat down. The five of them spent hours reading and talking.

"Is this the only copy you have?" Joe asked. Marco nodded. "Is there someplace we can make a copy of it?"

"Yep, I can take it to my office," Charlie offered.

"Why don't I go with you? If you're being watched, we can't let them know you have this."

"Hey, take the scanner. Check his office first. "Al handed Joe the scanner. Marco, Beckett, and Al went back to the room while Elizabeth made it look like everything was normal. Marco knew their life would never be normal again. He knew that there was a great chance that he and Beckett were going to have to leave Bells Harbor to start new lives with new names, in a new town. It's not what he wanted to do.

"The director of the F.B.I. in D.C. is a friend of mine. We did a job for him a few years back. I want to take that file to him. He is the only one I would trust."

Marco nodded. "But what about the family?"

"Well, I'm pretty sure it would be like a house of cards. Jay is a good man, and he knows his job. I'm sure he'll be able to take care of the family once we get Brick out of the way. I'm still finding it hard to believe that Julian is dead."

"What?" Beckett snapped. "Do you think he's not?"

"Well, I'm finding it a bit hard to swallow. Brick would have made sure you paid for it if he was. I've been kept up to date on Brick over the years, waiting for the moment I could take him down."

Beckett looked at Marco. "Maybe that's why the gun he gave me was loaded with blanks."

"Brick gave you guns?" Al interrupted her. She nodded, pulling the one from her jeans and then getting the other one he gave her from under the bed, handing them to Al. She watched as he examined them. "These are rigged to backfire."

"Meaning what?" Marco asked, handing him the one he had.

"Meaning if you were to pull the trigger, you would be the one who got shot."

Beckett looked at Marco. "I don't care if I go to prison for the rest of my life; if I see that man again, I'm going to kill him."

Al laughed, looking at Marco. "She's got spunk."

Marco smiled. "She spent twenty years being beaten by Julian. She won't get the chance to kill him."

"Oh, you don't own me, Marco Lucian."

He laughed. "No, I don't, but I love you." Her eyes softened.

"When Joe gets back, I'll get you some guns. We've discussed a plan to bring Brick to you. Take him that way. I'm not sure how deep this is, but Joe's father-in-law is a senator, and I'm sure he'd be able to get some information. This may take some time, but we'll get it done."

The door clicked open, and Charlie and Joe walked in. Joe handed Marco the file, looking at Al as he said, "His office was wired with sound and cameras. I called the guys; they are bringing all the toys. They should be here later tonight." Looking at Marco, he said, "I'm going to do this only because Brick needs to be stopped. For too long, he's been getting away with this. You two stay put; we've got work to do."

Marco nodded as Al stood. He pulled his gun, handing it to Marco. "I'll be back."

As the door closed behind them, he grabbed Beckett, pulling her onto his lap, nearly crushing her. "Fuck, Beck."

"I know," she whispered.

Days passed as Marco and Beckett stayed hidden. They kept the TV on, watching the news, and they spent a great deal of time sleeping.

Al had come back, and Charlie opened the door. "You two ready?" Al asked. "We've got your house and cabin wired. We are thirty strong. Brick has been busy taking the family down. Most of them are dead. He's using his position to justify the killings. Jay's been keeping us informed. Brick's been talking to someone outside the agency, using burner phones because we can't seem to get a line on them. I don't think the family is worried about you right now. They are pretty much trying to avoid being gunned down."

Beckett grabbed Marco's arm. "Something's not right." She reached for the file. They stood there watching her flip through the pages, stopping when she got to the photographs. Taking them out, they watched as she carefully laid them on the floor. Marco smiled as she studied each picture. It was when she closed her eyes that his heart started to race. She was remembering.

Al touched his arm, whispering, "What is she doing?"

Marco chuckled. "She has an eidetic memory. She's remembering."

The four of them stood there watching her. She moved a few pictures around, closing her eyes. When they opened, she looked right at Marco. He could see the light in them. Her smile was slow as it stretched across her face. "I was there, at least three of the eight times." She picked up one of the pictures. "I was in that car." She pointed to the car in the distance. "I had no clue who he was, and I couldn't see his face. But this is Julian."

"Do you know where this is?" Al asked, taking the picture.

"They were all taken at the same place, and yes, I know where this is. Julian had a section of an old warehouse turned into... into this place where they would all have sex. He would take me there and make me watch, so I would know what was expected of me when we were married."

"Did you ever see Brick there?"

"No, it was always just Julian and his crew."

"Do you know how to get there?" She nodded, then proceeded to tell Al. "All right, stay put. I'll be back."

Marco touched Charlie's arm. "How long have we been down here?"

"Ten days. Elizabeth is going shopping in the morning to replenish your supplies."

"Charlie, we need to get out of here. Al said my house is secure. We can go there."

He nodded, moving to the door. "Al," he called. Al came back. "Marco wants to go back to the cottage."

Al looked at Marco. "To be honest, I'll need at least ten men to look after you. Trust me, the safest place right now is here. A few more days and this should be over." Marco nodded, and Charlie closed the door.

Beckett picked up the remote, turning on the TV. She climbed on the bed, pulling her knees to her chest.

"What's going on in that head of yours? I was watching you. Beck, talk to me."

Her eyes moved, locking with his. "Something's not right. I can't put my finger on it, but something is wrong. I just need to be in my head for a little bit."

He smiled at her. Picking up the file, he got comfortable in the chair.

Beckett closed her eyes, letting the scene play out in her head.

"Get your ass in the car, Beckett," Julian said to her.

"I'm not going with you."

He grabbed her arm, pulling her hard to his chest. "Yes. You. Are."

"Julian, you're hurting me."

"I'm going to do a hell of a lot more if you don't get in the fucking car." He shoved her into the car.

Beckett slammed into the other door. Opening it, she got out. "I'm not going," she yelled.

Julian grabbed her around the waist, lifting her off the ground. "Why do you make me hurt you?"

"Kill me!" she screamed. "I would rather be dead than watch you and your mongrels fuck."

He grabbed her hair and pulled her to him, kissing her. She tried to push his face away, and he pulled back, laughing. "Oh, my sweet little Beckett. You need to learn what I like in the bedroom. You already suck my cock so perfectly."

"It's not you in my dreams, it's..."

He slapped her. "Say his name to me and you won't walk for a week."

Beckett spit in his face, which only fueled his rage. Dropping her on the driveway, he grabbed her hair and dragged her to the car. She fought him, screaming the whole time. When he threw her in the car, she hit her head and was knocked out.

Julian poured a bucket of cold water on her to wake her up. Coughing and trying to catch her breath, she realized she was strapped to a chair in a room with a glass wall between her and the people having sex.

Julian grabbed her hair, pulling her head back. "You will watch, and you will learn."

"Fuck you!" she screamed at him.

An unknown voice behind her startled her. "You should just fuck her."

Beckett watched Julian smile. "She will remain a virgin until she becomes my wife. Then I'm going to fuck her to death."

The voice laughed. "I'd pay money to see that."

"You got it." Julian laughed.

The hand came from behind her, shaking Julian's. Beckett saw the man's watchband and a tattoo of what looked like a heartbeat on the inside of his wrist.

Beckett's eyes flew open, and she was moving off the bed toward Marco. She took the file from him. He sat there watching her go through page after page. When she stopped, she mumbled, "Son of a bitch. I can't believe I missed this."

"What?"

Turning, she handed him a picture. "Your father knew what he was doing. Marco, I'm starting to believe he planned all of this. Me, you, this whole thing."

"Beck, what am I looking at?"

"What do you see?"

"I see Julian shaking hands with someone. What do you see?"

She giggled. "I see a hand with a watch on it."

He chuckled, wrapping his arm around her. "This could be my wrist." He showed her his wrist with his watch on it.

"It could," she turned his wrist around, "but you don't have a tattoo here." Her fingertips ran along his pulse point.

His breath hitched. Turning, he picked up the picture, looking more closely. "How the hell did you see that? Who is it? Do you know?"

She nodded. "Everything gets stored in my brain. It takes things sometimes to trigger the memory. This particular memory you don't want to know, but that wrist was less than four inches from my face. I didn't connect the dots until just now. But I have recently seen that same wrist."

Marco's heart sped up, and his mouth went dry. "Beck?"

She smiled, moving closer, her lips nearly touching his. "Where are you taking me on vacation?" Her breath was warm. "I want to go someplace warm, Mr. Miller. Really warm. Hot." Her lips touched his, her kiss sweet and slow.

Marco didn't resist her, he couldn't. Dropping the picture on the floor, he grabbed her thighs. Lifting her. he moved to the bed, laying her down with Beckett's legs still wrapped around him. Marco pressed himself against her core. "Mmm... again," she moaned. He didn't disappoint her.

Pulling back, he watched her as he pressed into her again. Her body quaked as his hand moved her shirt up her chest, exposing her perfect breasts. Cupping one, he gently pinched her nipple as he pressed into her again. Marco couldn't believe what he was feeling as her whole body shattered into a beautiful orgasm. The blush that covered her alabaster skin nearly caused him to release.

"So beautiful," he moaned as he devoured her mouth. Marco slowed his assault on her mouth, gently pulling her shirt down, and touching her face. "Tell me who is in the picture."

She busted out laughing and pushed on his chest, and he rolled over onto his back as she got up. Her eyes landed on his erection bulging in his jeans.

He was watching her as she moved her hand back to touch him. She hesitated, but he didn't stop her when she pressed her hand on him. "Oh my," she whispered.

He moved his hand to cover hers, pressing harder. "It's because of you." His words were kind. "No one but you." He wanted her to understand that Katherine was not in his mind, only her.

She smiled, pulling her hand away. Beckett moved off the bed, picking up the photo. "The watch, the wrist, and the tattoo belong to Brick."

"How can you be sure?"

"When he gave me the gun, I saw it."

"We need to get in touch with Al," Marco said. Getting off the bed, he moved to the switch and flipped it. When he turned around, the bathroom door was closing.

A few minutes later, the door clicked open, and Charlie and Al walked in, closing the door behind them.

"What's going on?" Al asked, just as the bathroom door opened.

Beckett smiled. "I'm done being locked away. This isn't living." Looking at Al, she said, "You said Brick was your boss at one time." He nodded. "Well, how well do you know his body?"

Al stood there looking at her. "I'm sorry, I don't understand the question."

"Does he have any tattoos?"

"A few, why?"

"Tell me about them." She sat on the bed.

"He has a few on his chest, one on his arm, and one on the inside of his wrist that looks like a heartbeat printout. Why?"

Beckett picked up the picture. "The man in this photo shaking hands with Julian is Brick." She handed Al the photo.

He stood there looking at it. "Son of a bitch. How did you see this?"

"It's a long story, but you are right. Brick is in this up to his eyeballs, and I'm the proof. That's why he gave me a gun full of blanks. It's why he kept the bloody clothes I was wearing when I stabbed Julian. I don't want to live my life in fear anymore. I want you to take me back to Chicago so I can end this, one way or another. Charlie and Elizabeth shouldn't be involved. Marco either. This is on me."

"No!" Marco shouted.

Beckett giggled and calmly said, "You don't own me, Marco. No one does. I'm tired. Twenty years is a long time to fight, a long time to be afraid. I'm so done. I'm going, and you are not going to stop me."

His eyes softened. "Then I'm going with you."

Al smiled. "Give me a few hours to make some arrangements. I'll be back."

Beckett sat on the bed, Marco in the chair. Neither of them said a word. Beckett laid down with her back to him. She was tired. Tired of the struggle to stay alive. All she'd ever wanted was to join him in death. Now, here she was with the man she had loved her whole life, and they didn't stand a chance in hell of having any kind of life together. She was struggling to understand the reasons why her life was this mess. What were her parents thinking, doing this to her? It was so unfair. She was glad she'd made the decision to sterilize herself. She never wanted to do this to a child. "My life is so fucked,"

she said softly. "When I turned twenty-one, I paid a doctor twenty-five thousand dollars to make sure I could never have children. That's how fucked up I am. There is nothing waiting for me. My father made Julian the trustee to my inheritance. He took everything from me." Marco sat there listening to her, his heart breaking. "I'm not going to sit here like this. Those fuckers are going to pay for what they did to me. I'm going to kill Brick."

The door clicked and then opened. Al walked in, but Beckett didn't move. He had a bag in his hand, and when he set it on the bed, he smiled at her. "Clothes that will fit you, along with a petite Kevlar that you will be wearing like it's your skin." Beckett took the bag and changed. When she walked out of the bathroom, Al smiled. "I have a few things for you." He handed her a hair tie. "Put this in your hair." Then he gave her a bead. "This goes in your shoelace." He handed her a pair of tennis shoes. "This one goes in the small pocket in your jeans. They are trackers." Beckett did what he said. Then he handed her a small knife. "Slip it inside the waistband of your jeans." Then a gun. "One in the chamber, seventeen in the clip, guaranteed not to misfire." She took the gun, slipping it in the back of her jeans. He handed her four more clips, and she smiled as she put them in her pockets. "You ready?" She nodded, and they left the security of Charlie's safe room.

Marco was silent, watching her gear up. He had an idea of what her life was like, but not really. He watched the girl he loved a long time ago arm herself. She was going to battle with the Devil, and there wasn't a thing he could do to stop her. This was the end for both of them, and he knew it. Charlie hugged him extra hard. Marco held back his tears; he knew he would never see the man who raised him into adulthood again.

On the plane, he sat alone watching her, listening to Al and Joe making their plans. Closing his eyes, he tried to concentrate on something other than what was happening. For the past year, he'd struggled, trying to understand why he survived. He struggled not to join them. He felt a tear slip from under his eyelid as a hand touched his leg. She wiped his tear. "Please understand," she whispered.

"I do, Beck."

"Then why the tears?" she whispered.

"For over a year, I wanted nothing more than to be with them. And now..." His voice trailed off. He wasn't sure it mattered anymore because he knew he would give his life to save her.

"And now?"

Marco looked at her for a long time before he answered. "And now, I want a life with you. I don't want to die. I don't want you to die." He slid his hands up her back, pulling her closer. She wrapped her arms around his neck, laying her head on his shoulder. They sat like that until the plane slowed down and started its descent into Chicago.

Beckett and Marco watched as the plane landed and then taxied into a hangar. When they got off, Al ushered them into the middle SUV. Marco counted eight in all. Joe got behind the wheel, and Al sat in the passenger seat.

"Beckett, I need you to talk to my man in the lead car. Tell him where to go, to the warehouse."

"I want Brick," she said softly.

"We need to set up for him. I want it all on film."

"The place is already wired. Everything that was done there was recorded."

Al looked at Joe, who said, "This is impossible, Al."

Beckett shook her head. "I'll be the bait. Call Jay. Tell him we are here and where we are. He won't kill me in front of everyone. He'll come; he knows I can identify him."

Al handed her a two-way radio. Marco didn't say a word. He knew people were going to die today. Beckett directed them to the warehouse. The cars stopped a few blocks away. Marco watched in silence as the cars emptied and the men scattered, disappearing into the dusk of probably the last day of his life.

"Can you guys give us a minute?" Marco asked. Al and Joe got out of the car. Marco sat looking at his hands, Beckett looking at him. "No matter what happens, I want you to know, I want you to feel in your heart that I love you."

Beckett put her hand on his. "I'm sorry for all the horrible things I said to you before. Thank you for everything you've done helping me."

"Beck—."

"Marco, don't. Please, just don't." She opened the door and got out of the car. Al turned to look at her. "Can I use your phone?" Al handed it to her. She dialed, watching Marco get out of the car. "Mr. Munch, this is Beckett Angelo. I'm in the warehouse district on LaClair Avenue. I was wondering if you could come and talk to me. I have some information I think you might need." She hung up and handed the phone to Al. "They'll be here shortly. You should go." She moved to get in the car, then looking at Marco, she said, "You coming? This will only work if we are both here."

Shaking his head, he got in the car. Fear was spiking his adrenalin as she drove the four blocks to the warehouse, stopping the car in the middle of the street. "I have always loved you. I will love you in death." Turning off the car, she opened the door.

Marco grabbed her, kissing her hard. She nodded, and they got out. Beckett sat on the hood, and Marco stood between her legs as they waited.

CHAPTER FOURTEEN

With Joe and Al, along with their crew of men stationed everywhere with high-powered rifles filled with tranquilizer darts, Beckett and Marco waited. They were the only two with guns loaded with bullets. It was silent as the day turned to night. Marco could hear his heart beating in his ears. He could feel Beckett shaking and closed his arm around her thigh.

Her head turned. "Here they come." Marco turned to look behind them and could see the headlights of the line of cars coming toward them. "I've loved you my whole life, Marco. Even in death, I have loved you and will love you."

"No one is dying here tonight, Beck."

She giggled. "There will be death here."

He turned to face her. Moving his hands to her face, he kissed her, whispering on her lips, "I love you, Beck." The slamming of car doors pulled them apart.

Marco watched Jay walk up. "Glad to see you're both alive. What are we doing here?"

"Where is your boss?" Beckett asked as she scanned the men approaching.

"I'm sure he'll be along." He smiled, nodding at Marco.

"This was Julian's sex house. The place was or is wired with cameras. Everything that happened in there," she nodded toward the warehouse, "was recorded. The files are in a computer bank in the security room. I think you'll find what you need in there."

Jay turned to look at the building. "Well, let's go."

Beckett giggled. "I'm not going in there. I have no desire." She reached in the pocket of her jacket, pulling out a piece of paper. "Here's a map of the layout with all the access codes to all the doors. We'll wait here."

Jay took the paper and looked at it. Then to two of his men, he said, "You two stay here with them."

"That's not necessary." Beckett smiled. "I have a guardian angel. We will be fine. Go get the evidence, Jay. I want to go on vacation."

He smiled, looking around at the buildings. Marco knew he was searching for Al and Joe. Jay nodded and walked away. Beckett and Marco watched the men descend on the warehouse and disappear inside. The street became eerily quiet.

"Why don't you get in the car and get warm? You're shaking."

She touched his face. "I'm fine for now." They just looked at each other, not saying a word. Beckett knew that the possibility that they were going to die there on that street was very real.

"You are so beautiful, Beck," he whispered to her.

She didn't say anything, just smiled a small smile. A few minutes later, she whispered, "Brick's here."

Marco moved his head to see two cars pull up. "He should have brought more men."

Beckett giggled. "I'm sure he did. Let's just hope Al's men took care of them." The car door slammed; Beckett flinched. She was going to kill him. "You ready?" she whispered. Marco nodded.

Brick walked up. "Beckett Angelo, you are under arrest for the murder of Julian Lucian."

Beckett giggled. "I'm sorry, Allen, but I'm making a citizen's arrest. You are under arrest for running a sex trade ring. For kidnapping and committing sexual acts on minors, for rape, and trafficking drugs." She busted out laughing at the look on his face. "I remember you,

186

Allen. "Although…" she got off the car, "I never saw your face, I did see this." She grabbed his arm, exposing his wrist, his tattoo. "You see, Allen, Julian's father found out about you in the end. He left us a secret file with pictures and information, which, by the way, is in the hands of your boss, the Director of the F.B.I."

Brick ripped his arm away from her and stepped back. It was a scene from a movie as he drew his gun, just as Beckett and Marco drew theirs. The men surrounding them fell to the ground one by one. Brick made the mistake of moving his eyes off Beckett. She didn't hesitate when she pulled the trigger, unloading her clip into his chest, knocking him to the street. When she finished, she released the clip and loaded another. Walking up to him, she put a bullet in his head, then dropped her gun and started to shake.

Marco grabbed her into his arms as she burst into tears. "Come on." He moved them to the car, holding on to her until she calmed down. Opening the door, he put her in the front seat and turned the engine on. He went and picked up the guns, setting them on the hood of the car. His eyes stayed on Beckett. She just shot a man in the head. A small smile crossed his lips. It was over now. She was free. He was free.

He heard footsteps. Turning his head, he expected to see Al and Joe, so he was stunned at the silhouette moving toward him in the darkness. The figure was tall and thin. His eyes moved to the gun. A voice he hadn't expected came out of the darkness.

"I wouldn't do that, brother." He turned his head as Julian stepped into the light. "You should have stayed dead, you fucking little prick. Now, you are going to die for touching what's mine, again."

Marco turned to face him, his hand moving behind him, gripping the handle of the gun stuffed in his jeans.

Beckett had opened her eyes, but she couldn't see Julian, only Marco. She watched as he gripped the gun. Then she heard him.

"She's my wife, not yours. She never was."

For Marco, what happened next happened in slow motion. He heard the click as Julian pulled the hammer back on the gun, just as Beckett ran past him, yelling as the gun went off. Marco watched in horror as Beckett's body jerked backward, falling to the pavement. Julian started screaming. Marco pulled the gun and fired it, hitting his brother in the head. He could hear his voice yelling as he dropped to the street, grabbing Beckett in his arms. His eyes filled with tears. "No, Beck."

He watched her eyes flutter open. "You're free now," she choked out, and her body went limp in his arms.

Marco shook her, screaming her name, but there was nothing.

Al, Joe, and another man came running up. "Marco, let her go. This is Doc; let him check her out.

Marco gently laid her down, moving to her head. His heart hammered in his chest and tears blurred his vision as he watched in silence.

"Shit," Doc said. "The bullet went straight through the Kevlar." He rolled her over, and Marco saw the blood on the pavement. Shaking his head, he couldn't comprehend what he was seeing. Doc opened her coat, ripping the blood-soaked shirt off. Then he undid the vest. As he lifted it off her body, Marco saw the bullet hole; it was in the center of the sugar skull she had tattooed on her heart. The scream that escaped him and ripped through the night made everyone jump. He stood, moving toward Julian, and lifted his gun, emptying it into his chest. Dropping his arm, he felt a hand on his shoulder.

"Marco, I'm sorry, man. She's gone."

He stood there like a zombie, watching the scene before him play out. The ambulances, the police cars, it seemed to take forever to end.

Jay stayed with him until her body was loaded into the ambulance and taken away. "Do you want me to call Charlie?"

"No. Just end this."

"We've got everything we need. It's done."

Marco left Chicago, but he didn't go back home. He couldn't, not with the memories of Katherine and his babies and Beckett there to haunt him. His life had been ripped to shreds. He wasn't sure he would ever recover.

Jay had gotten word to him that he was the sole heir to his father's fortune. He donated it to help find children who were sold into the sex trade.

He made his way to the Cayman Islands where he took the untainted money his parents left him. He sent Charlie a check for a million dollars and never went back to the States. He never went home again. Home is where the heart is, and his heart was now a cold stone in his chest.

EPILOGUE

ONE YEAR LATER

Marco stood on the beach looking at the pictures of Katherine, Angela, and Beckett. The last two years of his life had nearly ended him, twice. He lost everything, nearly drowning him. He wasn't sure what to expect coming here, but this was his life now.

When Marco went to the bank, he discovered that the money had grown over the twenty years it was there. Inside a safety deposit box, he found a man's name. Discovering the man was a lawyer, he went to see him.

His parents had purchased a small resort on the beach and put it in his name.

Turning, he looked at the white sprawling resort with people milling about. Guests lounged on the beach. He was learning how to run the place. It had been making money for years. A small smile crossed his lips. "If it ain't broke, don't fix it," he mumbled. Looking at the pictures again, he smiled. "I will always love you."

He wasn't going to just exist anymore. He needed a purpose. Heading back to his office, he made his way through the resort, smiling at the guests, talking to a few, when a beautiful woman that felt very familiar to him walked up.

"Hi, are you Mr. Miller?"

He chuckled. "I am. Can I help you with something?" He noticed she wasn't dressed like the other guests. Her outfit caused him to think of Kate.

"Sherry, she works the front desk, well, she told me that you were looking for a personal assistant."

Marco smiled at her. "I don't do the hiring, Miss...?"

"Oh, I'm sorry, my name is Kate Ellis." She put her hand out to shake his, but he just stood there looking at her. Her name threw him off balance.

"I'm sorry. Please, excuse me." Turning, he walked away. His phone vibrated in his pocket, and he pulled it out. "Marc Miller."

"Mr. Miller, this is Jacob at the front desk."

"What can I do for you?" He turned to look at the woman who had approached him. She was walking away from him.

"A woman checked in this morning, and she just headed out toward the pool."

Marco chuckled. "Why are you telling me this?" He looked down at the flower bed.

"Well, sir, she asked if you were here and where she could find you."

Marco chuckled. "Yeah, I think she found me. She's looking for a job."

"No, sir, when I asked the woman her name, she said she was your wife." His head jerked as he watched the woman walk out onto the sand. She turned and smiled at him. Marco's heart stopped. He couldn't breathe. "Kate," he whispered. She waved as her image faded in the sunlight.

"Mr. Miller?"

The words were strangled and low as he forced them out of his mouth. "I'm not married." His eyes moved to the ring he wore on his left hand. The ring he bought that day after Julian's funeral. He just stood there. A movement of blue color fluttered in the breeze; his eyes moved from the ring to the blue cloth. His breath hitched in his chest. The phone in his hand dropped to the ground. He could feel his body shaking as he tried to focus on the woman standing less than five feet from him. Her smile was slow across her lips as his tears blurred his vision.

"Hi, husband." Her voice was soft, her eyes filling with tears. "Did you miss me?" she whispered.

"I saw you die." His voice was so low he wasn't sure he spoke.

"I did," she whispered.

"But how?" She stepped forward. "No, you're not real."

Her hands moved to her blouse, and he watched as she unbuttoned it. Marco stood shaking his head as she moved the material away. His eyes left her face, moving to the exposed skin. Blinking the tears away, his eyes cleared as he focused on the small tattoo on her left chest, the sugar skull with a pink scar in the center of it. His eyes jerked back to hers. "Beck?"

She nodded, taking another step. "Yes."

He reached out, wrapping his hand around her neck. "But how? Where have you been?"

"Al, Joe, and Jay. I needed to testify. It's over now. I needed you to be free."

Her hand came up to rest on his chest. He felt her. Closing his eyes, he took a deep breath. "Beck," he sighed on her lips.

"Marco," she whispered as he kissed her.

www.ingramcontent.com/pod-product-compliance
Lightning Source LLC
Chambersburg PA
CBHW020622180626
46810CB00007B/2900